ACCURSED SPACE

STAR MAGE SAGA BOOK 5

J.J. GREEN

TABLE OF CONTENTS

1

C arina Lin was hanging upside down by her knees in the *Duchess*'s gym when she received a message via her ear comm that the scanners had picked up Lomang's inter-sector vessel.

She pulled herself up to grab the bar, crunching her aching gut one more time. After unhooking her legs she jumped down to the mat and then walked toward the exit, grabbing a towel to wipe the sweat from her neck.

"Where are you going?" Atoi asked, hanging from the same bar. "Wimping out already? I thought you wanted to get into shape?"

"After two months with you as my workout partner," Carina replied, "I think I'm pretty much *in* shape. We can't *all* be stronger than half the men aboard, you know."

"Yeah, whatever," Atoi said before muttering, "*Lightweight.*"

Carina smiled and stepped through the opening gym doorway. Then she turned back to her friend and called out, "You'd better make the most of your session. You're gonna be on duty for the next few cycles."

Atoi's eyes widened in her flushed, puffy, upside-down face.

"We found the smuggler's ship?" She gave a whoop, reached up to grab the bar and then kicked off from it, somersaulting onto the mat. "Earth, here we come!"

Carina strode quickly toward the mission room, where Cadwallader was waiting, though her excitement was giving way to tension. Meeting with the lieutenant colonel was something she'd been avoiding when she could ever since the 'incident' involving Sable Dirksen. But now the Black Dogs and she had the opportunity to take over the Lomang's ship, she would need to work closely with Cadwallader to coordinate the merc and mage attack.

When she entered the mission room, Cadwallader was seated at the holo screen. He didn't deign to look at her, let alone greet her.

The *Duchess*'s computer was building a translucent hologram of the inter-sector ship from the arriving scanner data. The image increased in detail by the second, refining the ship's lines and bringing the equipment on the hull into relief.

Two can play at that game, Carina thought, strolling over to the holo screen. She studied the interface display to discover the ship's dimensions. What she saw caused her to draw in a breath. She'd heard the starships that traveled the unimaginable distances across and between galactic sectors were big, but she hadn't realized just how big.

Lomang's ship was even larger than *Nightfall*, the Sherrerr's former flagship. According to the display, it measured 2889 meters in diameter at its widest point and its longest dimension was 3523 meters. Carina had heard that colony ships were massive, and she guessed that was its original purpose.

No thought had been put into making the ship pleasing to the eye. It was a mess of bumps and lumps, a bulky, hulking mass of dull metal resting motionless in the void.

From what she'd heard, most of the ship's capacity would be taken up by fusion engines but that still left plenty of room for living facilities. The extra space would make a welcome change from the cramped, overcrowded *Duchess*. Then there were the Deep Sleep capsules...

"It's equipped with defensive weaponry," Cadwallader said in his usual clipped tones. "It isn't a warship, but we should be cautious when approaching it nevertheless."

Carina sat down and looked upward at their target. The holo of the ship had begun to spin while the computer continued to add detail. She saw the armaments Cadwallader had referred to: lasers aimed at the docking ports and airlocks —presumably to deter illegal boarding—and plasma cannons spaced in three rough rings encircling the ship. These were short-range weapons intended to protect against take-over attempts, but, as Cadwallader had said, the inter-sector ship wasn't a military vessel. It wasn't carrying any long-range weapons. Perhaps these kinds of ships couldn't afford to expend the energy needed for their immense journeys on pulse cannons or particle beams.

"Lomang will have put safeguards in place before leaving it," said Carina. "If it's entirely unmanned, he might have set booby traps and the stars know what else. I'll Enthrall him and see what I can find out."

Cadwallader nodded, maintaining his lack of eye contact. "Do that. The *Duchess* is already slowing down. I'll wait to hear what he says before we proceed farther."

Carina stood up and went to leave, but she stopped. She'd endured Cadwallader's behavior toward her for longer than she cared to.

"Look, we're going to have to work closely on this. Don't you think it's time that we put aside our differences and—"

"Our *differences*?!" Cadwallader gaped, finally looking at her.

Then he got to his feet and slammed his hands on the holo screen table.

"You jeopardized the safety of my crew and effectively

banished me and the *Duchess* from this entire galactic sector, and you think we have a difference of *opinion*?"

Carina gritted her teeth. "I've already admitted I was too hasty in executing Sable Dirksen. I know I shouldn't have taken the decision out of your hands, okay? What else do you want me to say? She deserved to die after what she'd done. Surely you're not going to tell me you would have let her live after she tried to kill a child?"

"There are more things to consider when defying the Dirksen clan than yourself and your family, Lin," said Cadwallader tensely. "The Black Dogs was already on their hit list after it took on the Sherrerr assignment to rescue your brother. The Dirksens must have figured out by now that their leader's dead and *we* had a hand in it. Our future in this sector is over."

He leaned over the table and glared at her. "You had *no* right to make yourself judge, jury, and executioner of Sable Dirksen, no matter what she did. I did *not* agree to allow you to decide the fate of our prisoners. You broke our contract and now we're all suffering the consequences."

She couldn't deny the lieutenant colonel made some good points. The encounter with the Dirksen corvette and Commander Kee as they left Ostillon had sealed the Black Dogs' fate. They had finally escaped the corvette that had trailed them—thanks to Darius's Cloaking of the *Duchess*—but Commander Kee would not forget them or their ship in a hurry.

Cadwallader's profile was too high to escape the Dirksens' notice when they investigated their leader's capture and disappearance, and the *Duchess* was an easily recognizable liability. The mercs who remained aboard her were also at risk.

Those who hadn't wanted to embark on the years-long journey to Earth had already resigned and disembarked on a backwater planet. Providing they made up convincing stories about their past that didn't include the name 'Black Dogs' they should be fairly safe from the Dirksens.

Yet, on the other hand, many of the mercs who had stayed seemed happy to come along on the journey to Earth. Atoi, Brown, Jackson, and Halliday had all signed up for the mission. Apparently, the prospect of not seeing their families for decades, or perhaps ever again, didn't faze them. Perhaps for some, the Black Dogs was the closest thing they had to a family.

It had been that way for Carina.

Even sour-faced Chandu was sticking around, though Carina was less pleased about his presence, especially since the incident where he'd gotten fresh with Parthenia.

The *Duchess* remained nearly at capacity in terms of its military contingent, which was fortunate. The Black Dogs were dead mercs walking as far as the Dirksens were concerned. There would be no new recruits.

"Fine," said Carina, meeting Cadwallader's cold-eyed stare. "Hold onto your grudge. I've apologized and there's nothing more I can say or do. I don't regret what I did, if that's what you want to hear. Not for a second. I would do the same in the same circumstances, and I *will* do the same to anyone who tries to kill a member of my family."

She stalked toward the door. "I'll bring Lomang back here, so you can question him with me. You probably know more about the potential hazards on his ship than I do."

"I do," said Cadwallader, fixing her with his ice-blue gaze, "and the hazards aboard this ship, too."

2

L omang's cell sat next door to Calvaley's. The decision to bring the Sherrerr admiral along with them had been hard to make. It had been only after long discussion that Carina had agreed with Cadwallader that they had no other option. The Black Dogs had taken the Sherrerr assignment to rescue Darius, so the band was not the clan's enemy, but Carina and her siblings most definitely were. Or, at least, if not their enemies, strictly speaking, they were definitely on the Sherrerrs' 'most wanted' list.

The clan would be extremely keen to have mages under their control again, and Calvaley would naturally divulge everything he knew about them. The Sherrerrs would be very interested to hear all about Carina and her last-known whereabouts, as well as that of Stefan Sherrerr's children.

The fact that Carina had rescued the admiral from near death at the hands of the Dirksens wouldn't make any difference to him. Gratitude wouldn't influence his loyalty to his clan, or his belief that whatever heinous act it committed was excusable 'for the greater good', as Carina had once heard him say.

She strode past Calvaley's cell and only glanced inside. The old man seemed to have mostly recovered from his ordeal of captivity and starvation. He'd put on weight and was looking healthy. Perhaps, when they had traveled so far, the possibility of him ever causing them any harm had faded to zero, they would release him.

Lomang, on the other hand, had continued to lose weight over the months he'd been incarcerated. Carina hadn't seen him for several weeks, and now he was almost down to the size of an average adult male. Next to his giant brother he looked positively shrunken. The cheeks that had once been round and full now hung loose, sagging around his jaw, making his large white teeth look as if they belonged to a gnawing animal.

Not that Lomang had allowed his predicament to dampen his confidence or panache. He greeted her with a wide grin. He sported his iridescent blue hat at an angle as if it were the latest fashion, though in truth the headgear was beginning to look worn and dull.

From what Carina had heard, he passed a lot of his time telling stories to Pappu. The brothers would also play cards their guards had given them as a gesture of kindness.

The smuggler's apparent sanguinity in the face of his adverse circumstances provoked a grudging respect from Carina.

Lomang seemed to return the sentiment, bowing low when she arrived outside his cell. Was his attitude sparked by the fact he'd witnessed her Transport Sable Dirksen to her death in the airless void outside the ship? Carina didn't dwell long on the question. All she needed from him was information.

"Ah, the mage queen has come to pay us a visit, Pappu," said the smuggler as he caught sight of Carina approaching his cell. "Stand up, stand up. Don't slouch in the presence of greatness."

Pappu was sitting on the cell floor, resting an arm on Lomang's bunk, one of his long, brawny legs outstretched. He climbed smoothly to his feet. For all the time the giant had spent in captivity, he didn't seem to have lost an ounce of muscle or tone. From the look of his abs under his thin shirt, Carina imagined that punching him would be like punching a wall.

Ignoring Lomang's attempt at flattery, Carina lifted her flask of elixir from its pouch in her belt.

"Oh, no, no, no," Lomang exclaimed. "Not the bewitching again. Please don't do that, sweet madam. I dislike the sensation intensely. It is most unpleasant. Just ask me whatever you want to know. I promise I will tell you whatever you like. I am an unsecured data base."

While Lomang babbled, Carina swallowed a large mouthful of elixir. She wanted to Enthrall both the men at once. The guards would have to remove Lomang in Pappu's presence and she didn't want the latter to try to escape.

She made the Cast. When she opened her eyes, the gazes of the smuggler and his brother had become vacant.

Carina asked the guard to open the cell and bring Lomang out. The smuggler didn't resist as he was escorted by his arm to her side. She told him to follow her and led him through the *Duchess's* corridors.

Before she reached the mission room, however, she saw Bryce approaching from the opposite direction.

"Hey," he said when they reached each other. "I heard we found the ship." Then, glancing at the smuggler, he asked, "Another interrogation?"

"I prefer to think of it as an interview," Carina replied innocently. "Under duress."

Bryce chuckled. "Just as long as you never do that to me. I don't want you finding out all my secrets."

"I already know them all."

"That's what I want you to think," said Bryce. He quickly kissed her on the lips. "I hope you find out what you want to know. I'll catch up with you later. I also have some exciting news to share."

Wondering what 'news' Bryce could have heard within that region of rarely traveled, uninhabited space, Carina continued taking Lomang to Cadwallader.

She arrived, the Enthralled smuggler still in tow, and found that Cadwallader's temper hadn't improved while she'd been gone. He didn't say a word as she walked into the room.

He was standing with his hands clasped behind his back, peering at the holo of the inter-sector ship. Details and definition were no longer being added to the model. The ship's scan was complete.

"Sit down," Carina instructed Lomang.

The man mechanically obeyed.

She set her ear comm to record.

"Right," said Cadwallader, also taking a seat. "Lomang, what is the name of this ship?" Cadwallader pointed at the holo.

"It is called the *Bathsheba*," the man replied in a monotone.

"And what defensive measures have you taken to prevent the *Bathsheba* from being stolen?" asked Cadwallader.

When Lomang struggled to answer, Carina said, "You should probably be more specific."

The lieutenant colonel threw her a sour look. "List all the traps you have set aboard your ship, the *Bathsheba*."

Carina listened carefully to the smuggler's reply, which included explosive devices set to go off in the airlocks if particular codes were not keyed in and the requirement to input his bio signatures to the ship's computer before initiating the engine start-up sequence, to avoid triggering a self-destruct.

Cadwallader asked more detailed questions about each trap, noting down the codes and other information, but Carina was listening to discover if he could be fighting the effects of the Enthrall and omitting something significant. She didn't get the impression he was. He explained each trap fully.

As Lomang himself was at risk of death when boarding the inter-sector ship with the mercs, Carina guessed he would have spilled the beans about them anyway.

She was interested in other potential dangers the Black Dogs would face when assuming control of the *Bathsheba*. "Lomang, what other dangers do we face if we board the ship?"

"Lasers are aimed at the ports and airlocks," the smuggler replied.

"We know about those," said Cadwallader. "What else is there to prevent us from assuming control of the *Bathsheba*?"

Lomang's lips remained closed and he stared directly ahead. Carina gazed into the man's eyes. He appeared to remain entirely Enthralled.

"There doesn't seem to be anything else," said Cadwallader.

"No, there doesn't," Carina said, but hesitantly.

She couldn't help feeling they were missing something.

For the next half an hour or so, she and Cadwallader continued to probe Lomang, but they learned little more than they'd gleaned in the first five minutes of questioning.

Then the smuggler began to show signs of throwing off the effects of the Enthrall. He blinked and appeared to try to focus his eyes.

"Hmpf," said Cadwallader. "Time for him to go back to his cell."

"Yes," Carina agreed. "I'll take him."

She told Lomang to go with her.

As she walked with him en route to the brig, she asked softly, "Are you hiding something, you old crook?"

Lomang only blinked.

3

After returning Lomang to his cell, Carina encountered Bryce again in a corridor.

"Are you stalking me?" she asked teasingly.

Bryce smiled. "You're an irresistible attraction."

"So, what's this news you want to tell me? You clearly can't wait."

"Well..." He put his hands on her waist. "Mmm. You really *are* irresistible, you know." He pulled her toward him and they kissed.

Carina utterly relaxed in his arms. She loved these moments they stole together, which were too few and far between.

Some time later, Carina heard Atoi say, "Ewww. For stars' sake, get a cabin."

She was watching them, hands on hips, shaking her head.

Laughing, they broke their embrace.

"We *have* a cabin," Bryce protested. "It's full of kids."

"Then do it in the mission room during the quiet shift like any other self-respecting crew member." Atoi strode away, still shaking her head.

Pulling Carina close again, Bryce said, "As soon as we're aboard the inter-sector ship we'll be able to have our own cabin, right? I've seen how big it is. The living quarters must be huge."

"Yeah, I'm sure they are," Carina replied. Then she added, with regret, "but I guess Darius and Nahla are still going to want to sleep with us."

Ever since escaping the *Nightfall* and their mother dying, Darius had always preferred to sleep near Carina. She'd never had the heart to discourage him. He was so young and he'd been through so much, it felt wrong to force him to sleep in his own bed.

And poor Nahla had been a mess of anxiety ever since witnessing Stevenson's death and being trapped in the pilot's cabin with his dead body. The little girl had lost all the bright cheerfulness she'd developed since escaping the control of her eldest brother, Castiel.

Bryce heaved a sigh. "I guess so. Still, we should be able to get some privacy sometimes, right?"

"Yeah, we should." Carina added, with concern, "Do you think Atoi was serious about the crew using the mission room for their trysts?" She'd begun to feel icky.

"You would have a better idea about that than me," said Bryce, pointedly.

A flicker of tension passed between them.

Was he going to bring up her history with the Black Dogs again? She thought he'd gotten over his jealousy.

"Anyway," he continued, "with all that space available, we should manage to finally get some time together. Just you and me."

"Yes, we should." Carina agreed.

The corridor was empty.

She leaned in for a kiss.

"We'll need to after we get married, after all," he murmured.

She paused. "What?"

"That was my news," Bryce said, his face centimeters from hers. His eyes were warm and happy. "I talked to Jace about it. He says he can perform the ceremony. He can marry us, mage-style. Isn't that great?"

Carina put her hands on his chest and moved her head back. "You talked to Jace about us getting married?"

"The subject kind of came up." Bryce chuckled and turned a little pink. "To be honest, I brought it up. That was what the Matching was for, after all, wasn't it? To find romantic partners. I thought to myself, mage tradition has to include a next step after the Matching. It turns out a mage wedding ceremony is pretty much the same as a regular one. You make promises to each other and then do some other stuff Jace said he would explain later. The best part is, he can officiate. He said he'd be happy to. Who would have thought, huh?"

"Yeah," said Carina. "Who would have thought?"

Bryce was studying her face. "What's wrong?"

"Nothing." She forced a smile. "I'm just a bit surprised. I hadn't really thought about us getting married yet."

"You hadn't?" Bryce asked. His arms fell to his sides and he took a step back. His happy expression had faded to unease. "Hadn't the idea even crossed your mind? I mean, I don't understand why not. We love each other. It's only natural we should get married."

"I do love you," said Carina. "But..."

Bryce's eyes grew serious as she struggled to complete her sentence.

Eventually, he said, "I thought we were on the same wavelength but clearly I was wrong. I've really sprung this on you, haven't I? But I don't understand, Carina. What is there to think about?"

She didn't have an answer. She didn't know if her reluctance was due to the days she'd spent as a merc, when no one got too close to anyone else, knowing the dangerous lives they were leading? Or perhaps it was Nai Nai's warning never to get involved with non-mages, which the old lady had drummed into her from as far back as she could remember. Or maybe it was a fear of what Bryce would be getting into, that he would be snatched from her and murdered, like Ba. She didn't know what exactly was holding her back.

"I guess there's a lot to think about," Bryce said, his expression a mixture of sadness, hurt, and disappointment.

She tried to think of something to say to reassure him, but nothing suitable sprang to her lips.

She felt like shit. After all Bryce had done and given up for her, she wanted to make him happy, but she also couldn't lie to him. The thought of the two of them getting married filled her with anxiety.

He went to say something, but an alert suddenly blared from the shipwide comm.

The *Duchess* was under attack.

"Crew to battle stations," ordered Cadwallader, his voice resounding along the passage. "The destroyer that severed us from the *Zenobia* is approaching. Prepare to engage."

They stared at each other. Carina wanted to hug Bryce before they parted to perform their duties. If the *Duchess* didn't survive the battle, they might never see each other again. But she hesitated. Their brief conversation had thrown a barrier between them.

She saw the same indecision in Bryce's eyes. Abruptly, he turned and strode away, heading for his station.

Hurt seared Carina's chest. She swallowed.

However, like Bryce, she also had a station she had to get to.

Unfortunately, it was on the other side of the ship. She set off, jogging toward the docking port, where she had to prepare to repel any boarders.

Damn Lomang's wife!

She'd been the danger the smuggler had managed to avoid mentioning. His wife had known the coordinates of his inter-sector ship, and she been waiting in the vicinity, perhaps in case Lomang managed to make it there, or in case the *Duchess* turned up.

Cadwallader had asked him, *What else is there to prevent us from assuming control of the Bathsheba?*

Not *who* else.

4

Carina had almost reached the docking port, when—
"Brace for acceleration," ordered a voice over the shipwide comm.

It took her a moment to recognize the speaker: it was the former co-pilot, Hsiao, who had taken over from Stevenson.

She scanned her surroundings for somewhere to prop herself against or something to hold onto before the *Duchess* sped up. Only the hand bars that lined the corridor just above head height—for use if the ship lost a-grav—were available.

She reached up, but just as her hand touched a bar the full acceleration force hit, flinging her along the passage and into a wall. Her skull and back smacked into the hard surface and air *whooshed* from her lungs.

The ship continued to move so fast she didn't slide to the floor but remained pressed against the wall.

Hsiao was really gunning it.

Struggling to breathe and trying to ignore the pain radiating from her head and spine, Carina hoped neither the kids nor Bryce had been hurt.

What was Cadwallader's reasoning behind the massive acceleration?

The last time the *Duchess* had faced Lomang's wife's ship, the fate of the battle had seemed sealed before it had even begun. The destroyer carried a particle lance, a weapon the mercs' vessel had little defense against. Pulse cannon fire could disrupt the particle beam somewhat, and a well-aimed shot could take out the lance, but at close quarters and unimpeded, a particle lance was deadly. A single direct hit, or rather 'slice', of a lance's beam would breach most ships' hulls.

Decompression would be fast and fatal to anyone unlucky enough to be caught in the path of the escaping air. Unlike the last time the *Duchess* had been hit by the lance, its occupants were not wearing EVA suits.

Had Cadwallader ordered Hsiao to try to outrun the destroyer? But the mercs' vessel didn't have the capability.

Then it hit her. The lieutenant colonel was trying to reach the *Bathsheba*. If the *Duchess* moved between the destroyer and the inter-sector ship, Lomang's wife might hesitate to fire, reluctant to risk damaging the larger vessel.

It was a smart move. In the circumstances, it was the only move.

Carina also had an idea what Cadwallader's end game was. If she was right, he would need her at her station.

She was pressed against a wall where the corridor turned around a corner. Grimacing at the effort, she twisted herself around and reached for the nearest handhold. Her fingers closed around the bar and she pulled herself forward against the force of acceleration, in the direction of the docking port. She gave out a grunt as she reached for the next bar, and the next, hauling herself hand over hand along the wall.

At the far end of the corridor, another merc appeared from an adjoining passage. He was also crawling along the vertical surface toward the port.

Cadwallader's voice barked from her ear comm, "Where are you, Lin? Why aren't you at your station?"

"On my way," she replied with some effort. "I'm trying, but—"

The lieutenant colonel cut her off. "Never mind. I need you there ASAP. I want you to lead a boarding party."

"A party to board the *Bathsheba*?"

"Unless you had somewhere else in mind?" Cadwallader's tone was sharp and sarcastic. "We've taken out the lasers defending one of the airlocks. ETA four minutes. Make it."

The comm went dead.

Shit.

Why her? Why not Atoi? As a captain, her friend was the obvious choice for the job.

Carina hoped Atoi hadn't been hurt, and that it was only that Cadwallader had another task in mind for her.

She grasped the next rung and pulled with all her strength. To run the distance to the port from her position would have only taken thirty seconds in normal conditions, but at the *Duchess*'s current acceleration she would be lucky to reach it in ten minutes.

Cadwallader had said she only had four. It was an impossible task.

She groaned as she dragged her body forward. By pushing her toes into the bars behind her she could propel herself onward a little and lessen the strain on her arms, which were already in agony. The sweat oozing from the skin on her hands also made gripping the handholds difficult.

The ship shuddered. It had been a hit.

Yelling echoed down the corridor. Someone was issuing orders, but she couldn't make out what they were saying. The *Duchess* must have received some damage.

How long had it been since Cadwallader had comm'd her? It had to be thirty seconds or even a whole minute.

The docking port remained frustratingly far away.

The merc ahead of her seemed to be barely moving too.

Another problem popped into Carina's mind: she wasn't in armor or carrying a weapon. According to Lomang's responses while Enthralled, the *Bathsheba* carried no crew, but his wife would probably also attempt to board the ship. If that happened a fight for control was a given.

An armory was situated near the port but reaching it would take additional time—time she didn't have.

Then she realized the flaw in her thinking. She'd been imagining the acceleration would continue, but if the *Duchess* sped up, that meant the ship also had to—

"Brace for braking," instructed Hsiao.

Carina quickly clutched two bars with all her might and scrabbled her feet around, trying to hook her toes under another bar.

The deceleration hit—hard.

When the reversal in forces came, her slippery hands couldn't hold onto the metal bars. As she flew down the passage, she lifted an arm to try to protect her head.

Her elbow took the full force of the impact.

She screamed as its bones shattered.

The deceleration was pushing her into the wall but it wasn't sufficient to hold her upright. She slid to the floor. Her right arm was strangely bent and blood soaked into her sleeve.

The other merc who had been trying to get to the port hit the wall beside her, but he was wearing armor that protected him.

He lifted his visor and pulled a face when he peered closer at Carina's wound. He slipped a knife from a sheath on his thigh and slit her sleeve open.

Bone shards were poking through her skin at her elbow.

"I'll comm for a medic."

"No," she gasped. "It's okay. Just..." she ground her jaw to prevent herself from crying out, "...just take the flask from my hip and pour some of the liquid into my mouth," she finished through clenched teeth.

The merc's eyebrows lifted but he did as she instructed.

The flavor of elixir was usually disgusting, but at that moment she didn't think she'd tasted anything more delicious.

She closed her eyes, forcing away the agony from her arm that threatened to consume her mind. She wrote the Heal Character in her mind's eye, and sent it out.

A second or two later, the pain began to fade.

She opened her eyes and looked at her elbow.

The bone shards had withdrawn into her skin, and the wound was closing up. Within a few beats her arm resumed a regular shape. Soon, all that remained of her injury was rapidly drying blood.

"Stars," breathed the watching merc. "I knew you could do magic but I didn't know you could do that."

"It isn't magic," said Carina irritably.

"*Shit*," she added, recalling Cadwallader's command. "We have to get to the docking port."

She screwed the lid onto her elixir canister, replaced it in its holster, and leapt to her feet.

The *Duchess* had continued to slow with brutal force while she'd been Healing herself, and the braking continued. *Good.* It meant they still had time before the ship attempted to dock with the *Bathsheba*.

She began to run, pressing her hand against the wall to counteract the rapid deceleration.

The armory appeared ahead of her, the doorway open. She ran inside, snatched one of the few remaining suits, and hastily put it on. Only two rifles remained. She grabbed one from its cradle.

As she'd been suiting up, the deceleration had eased.

"Lin," blurted Cadwallader from her ear comm, "where the hell are you?"

It was a rhetorical question. The lieutenant colonel knew exactly where she was. Her armor would have identified her from her bio signatures and logged her position in the ship's system.

"Nearly there, sir," she replied.

Sir? Where had that *come from?*

She'd automatically slotted back into merc mode, but there was no time to ponder it.

Carina sprinted out of the armory and headed for the port.

As she was running, the *Duchess* jerked violently, throwing her to her knees. Had the ship taken another hit?

Or maybe they hadn't been hit—maybe they'd clamped onto the *Bathsheba.*

She rounded the final corner and ran directly into a bunch of ten or more mercs in armor. The men and women were checking their weapons and lowering their visors.

Names appeared on her HUD, identifying the soldiers. Bryce was not among them, which wasn't surprising—his battle station was at the *Duchess's* airlock. Yet she found herself wishing he was there.

The mercs turned to face her, awaiting orders.

5

Parthenia opened the door to her cabin and peeked out. Mercenaries in full armor and holding pulse rifles across their chests were running past, all heading in one direction.

"What's happening?" Oriana asked, peering over Parthenia's shoulder.

"Oh!" She drew back as she caught sight of the soldiers. "Where are they going?"

"To the docking port, I think," Parthenia replied, annoyed. She pressed the button to close the door. "No one's told us anything. They've forgotten we exist."

"They have better things to do than give battle updates to a bunch of kids," said Ferne. He was lying on the bunk he shared with Oriana, his hands behind his head and his legs splayed out, taking advantage of having the entire bed to himself. "I'm just glad all that horrible accelerating and braking is over."

"We aren't *just* a bunch of kids," said Parthenia. "If there's a fight going on, why didn't they ask if we could help, like we did at the mages' mountain castle on Ostillon? It's as if Carina and the rest of the adults have forgotten all about everything we did."

"That was pretty awesome." Ferne grinned and sat up. "I reckon I Transported at least five Dirksen soldiers."

He mimed a throw. "Pow!" And then another. "Kerpow!"

"It *was* exciting," Oriana said, "until Darius got hurt."

"Oh, yeah." Ferne's face fell. "I forgot about that."

He looked at his little brother, who was sitting on the bunk opposite, playing a game on an interface with Nahla. "But you're okay now, right, Darius?"

"Yes, I'm all better now," the boy replied absently before quickly prodding the screen with a forefinger. "I got it!"

"You did!" Nahla squealed and clapped her hands. "Now it's my turn."

Darius handed over the interface.

"Maybe they didn't have time to ask us to help them," said Oriana. "I don't think they knew this battle was coming up."

"That's right," Ferne said. "What was it Cadwallader said? The same destroyer that attacked us before was going to attack again. I don't think they expected it would follow us all the way here, not after Darius Cloaked our ship."

"No, maybe not," Parthenia conceded. "But I feel so useless. I want to *do* something, not sit around in here like a pathetic baby while others risk their lives."

"Carina would want us to stay here, where we're safe," said Darius, not lifting his gaze from the screen Nahla now held.

"So?" Parthenia replied, irritably. She folded her arms across her chest. "We don't have to do what Carina says. She isn't our mother, and, anyway, I'm sixteen. I can make my own decisions."

Ferne mimicked her, folding his arms and waggling his head as he mouthed, *I can make my own decisions.*

Oriana chuckled and Darius and Nahla looked up to see what she was laughing at.

"Ferne!" Parthenia admonished. Then she smiled, stomped over to her bunk, picked up a pillow, and swung it at Ferne's head.

He threw his arms up, but he was too late. The pillow hit him full in the face. He curled onto his side in fits of giggles.

Parthenia's smile disappeared and she slumped onto Ferne's bunk. "This is serious. We should be doing something. *I* should be doing something, at least. I'm the eldest after Carina. All the soldiers are only here and fighting because they have to be, because she killed Sable Dirksen."

"It isn't our fault she did that, though, is it?" asked Oriana.

"I suppose not," Parthenia replied, "but I can't help feeling responsible somehow."

"You're always taking responsibility for things that aren't anything to do with you," said Ferne soberly. "Like you did with Castiel."

The mention of her brother's name only increased Parthenia's feelings of guilt and remorse. She'd been sure for so long that her Dark Mage brother was the family's problem to fix. Now, she wasn't so certain she'd been right, and she regretted constantly pushing Carina to bring him under control.

But she didn't think she was wrong to want to join in the current battle. Surely she should support the soldiers? She could do so much to help.

She stood up decisively and strode to the door.

"Where are you going" Darius asked, her sudden movement distracting him from his game.

She opened the door. "Out—for a while. You all stay here, okay? Don't leave this room unless you really have to."

"You're going to fight with the soldiers, aren't you?" said Ferne. "You're going to be in so much trouble."

But Parthenia didn't answer. The door was already closing behind her.

The corridor was empty and she couldn't hear a thing. Even the noise of the running mercenaries had faded away. She hesitated. Now that she'd decided to do *something*, she wasn't sure exactly *what*.

The deceleration of the *Duchess* had ended with an abrupt jerk. Had the ship connected with another vessel—perhaps the destroyer—and were the Black Dogs fighting the enemy?

Parthenia made up her mind and began to run toward the main armory. The fastest route would take her through the brig, so she headed in that direction.

An eerie silence reigned in the corridors. Even the steady, subliminal throb of the vessel's engines had stopped.

When she was growing up on Ithiya, she'd read tales of ghost ships—starships found drifting in space, entirely empty of passengers yet their distress signals inactivated. Whether the stories were true or not she couldn't guess, but she quickly found herself longing to see a human face to dispel the sense of creepiness setting in.

It was funny, having so many brothers and sisters often left her longing for some time alone, but actually being alone made her uncomfortable.

The brig came into view. As she'd predicted, only one soldier had been left behind to guard it. The sight of the woman was a relief in the nearly empty ship, and Parthenia wasn't worried about what was bound to happen next.

"Hey," the guard called out as Parthenia rapidly approached her, "where are you going?"

"Hi," she replied, giving a small wave. "I won't be long."

"Won't be long doing what?" the guard asked. "You can't—"

Parthenia reached her and sped right past the woman and into the brig.

"Just passing through," she said cheerily, over her shoulder.

She caught a glimpse of Lomang and his brother, and the

Sherrerr admiral, Calvaley, in the neighboring cell, staring at her as she flitted by, then she was through. The guard hadn't had time to react, and, after all, the woman couldn't fire on a *child*, could she?

A minute or so later, Parthenia arrived at the armory, breathless. She was confident her armor would still be in storage there. It had been specially made for her for the mission on Ostillon and wouldn't fit anyone else.

Though she was keen to join in the battle, even she knew it would be foolish to enter it wearing no armor.

She stepped through the entrance, and then jumped in surprise as she spotted a large, tall, dark figure standing with his back to her, rummaging in a storage unit. She'd expected the place to be empty like most of the rest of the ship.

"Jace!" she exclaimed, recognizing the man. "You gave me a shock."

He turned to face her. "Parthenia, what are you doing here?"

"I..."

Would he disapprove of her plan? Probably.

"I could ask you the same question," she said.

"I'm looking for armor," the mage replied. "Cadwallader told me to stay put, but I feel useless and pathetic sitting around while others are fighting...which is also why you're here, isn't it."

His final utterance was a statement, not a question. His gaze was fixed on Parthenia, stern beneath his black, bushy eyebrows.

She wilted a little under his stare, but then she rallied. She liked Jace a lot and she had plenty of respect for him—she'd spent many long hours with him learning about mage lore during the weeks of journeying to reach the inter-sector ship—but at the end of the day he wasn't her father and so had no right to tell her what to do.

"What if I am?" She marched into the room and over to a cupboard where the children's armor was stored. Carefully avoiding eye contact with Jace, she pressed her hand on the plate to open the unit and took out her armor.

The mage remained silent as she emptied her flask of elixir into the suit's reservoir. Perhaps he was weighing his words.

Finally, he said, "Parthenia, it would be remiss of me to allow you to take part in—"

"Then it's just as well you don't get a say in the matter," she retorted.

She slipped off her shoes and stepped into her suit's legs and boots.

Inwardly, she was wincing at her defiant words. She didn't want to offend Jace, but on the other hand, she had to make it clear she wouldn't let him order her around.

Unexpectedly, Jace snorted with laughter. "I can tell you and Carina are related."

"I don't know what *that's* supposed to mean," Parthenia snapped. She and her older sister were *not* alike. Carina was bossy and opinionated, and not similar to her at all.

She pushed her arms into her armor and hefted it over her shoulders. As the edges of the front came together they automatically joined and sealed.

Rather than answering her, Jace only scanned the storage unit and sighed. "I'm not going to find anything for me to wear. There's hardly anything left and what's here is too small."

"Then it wouldn't be wise for you to accompany me," she said sweetly.

The mage rolled his eyes. "Are your brothers and sisters alone?"

"Yes, I had to leave them, but they should be okay. Darius is a force to be reckoned with all by himself." She put on her helmet, its visor up, and it locked into place.

"Nonetheless," said Jace, "I think I'll go and stay with them.

It'll be something useful for me to do, and if the battle goes badly they might need me."

"The battle won't go badly," Parthenia said, grabbing a pulse rifle. "Not now Carina *and* I are fighting on our side."

6

Carina carefully copied the first of two lines of digits displayed on her HUD onto the keypad inside the *Bathsheba's* airlock. The numbers comprised one of the codes Lomang had given while Enthralled, and it was supposed to correspond with this particular entry point.

If she got the numbers wrong—or if Lomang had managed to fight the effects of the Cast sufficiently to give a wrong number—the airlock would explode.

Given time, they might have found the explosive devices and disarmed them, but they didn't have time. Lomang's wife was bearing down on them in her destroyer. At any moment she might attempt to blast the *Duchess* away from the prized inter-sector ship, or she might board the *Bathsheba* herself. She might know about the various booby traps Lomang had set and how to circumvent them.

Mercs crowded behind Carina, waiting to enter the foreign ship and defend it. She glanced at the twenty or so men and women Cadwallader had assigned to the task. Beyond them, she could see more arriving. It looked like the lieutenant colonel had committed most of the Black Dogs to the effort.

His decision made sense. The *Bathsheba* was massive. It would take more soldiers than they had to repel a boarding attempt.

And yet...

"Return to the *Duchess*," Carina ordered. "All of you. Step back to the other side of the port and seal it. Wait for me to reopen it from this side."

The soldiers hesitated.

One of them murmured, "But, if we—"

"Follow my order, dammit!" Carina barked.

With some apparent reluctance, the mercs shuffled out of the airlock.

The *Bathsheba's* entry hatch closed. She was alone.

If the airlock exploded there was a good chance only she would be killed, and the Black Dogs would survive to protect her brothers and sisters.

She inhaled and, holding her breath, she read the second line of digits on her visor display and then keyed them in, one by one. There were eight numbers in total. She pressed the keys seven times. She guessed she had to be inputting the digits correctly or she would have set off the explosives.

A bead of sweat crawled down the side of her face.

Every muscle in her body tight, she pressed the final key.

Nothing happened.

She exhaled.

Then she realized that though there had been no explosion, the airlock hadn't activated.

The numbers on the display above the keypad faded away and words in a script she didn't recognize appeared.

Perhaps her suit's computer could tell her what they meant. She focused her gaze on the words and asked for a translation.

A message popped up on her HUD: *Does not translate.*

Carina sighed.

All the information she had to go on was that the background to the display stayed green. Did the unchanging color mean she'd input the correct code? Assuming she had, why hadn't the airlock activated?

Or was it designed to be activated manually?

She stepped back from the keypad and scanned around the inner hatch for a lever, wheel, or something similar.

It was possible that the *Bathsheba's* operating devices might be as alien as its written language, but if the ship was designed to be operated by humans, surely she should be able to recognize what to press, pull, turn, or push to work the airlock?

But the surface around the inner door was entirely smooth except for a square recessed area at the bottom, flush with the floor.

She squatted down and squinted into the hollow space, which measured roughly fifteen centimeters square. It was empty inside, but the base sloped upward, making the rear of the hole smaller than the opening.

Puzzled, Carina stood up.

The message in an unknown language was unchanged and the airlock remained dormant.

Minutes were passing.

If Lomang's wife intended to board the *Bathsheba* she could be inside by now. It was vital the Black Dogs gained entry immediately.

But how?

The pressure of so many people depending on her was building up and she began to grow angry. She'd done what was required. Why wasn't the airlock working?

"C'mon," she muttered, and thumped the closed hatch with a fist.

She brought up the code on her HUD again and pressed the key of the first digit, but the number didn't appear on the display. The message remained stubbornly in place.

Shit!

Was the code she'd input right or wrong? What was the message saying? Was it a warning, telling her to leave?

She **had** to get inside the *Bathsheba* or Lomang's wife would get control.

Anger and frustration boiled up, and Carina kicked the hatch. Her leg muscles jarred as her boot impacted the hard surface. Cursing, she looked up and down the entrance to the inter-sector ship again. Her gaze alighted on the recess in the bulkhead and suddenly something clicked in her mind.

The hole was roughly the width and height of a booted human foot. The inclined base could be a kind of lever.

She put her right foot inside the hole, but before she pressed down, she paused.

What if attempting to activate the airlock after inputting the wrong code would trigger the explosives?

She cursed once more. If she didn't try, their cause was lost anyway.

She trod on the base of the hole.

It depressed, and she was surrounded by the sound of valves opening and air hissing through them.

The tension in her muscles released all at once and it was as much as she could do to remain upright. She leaned her forearms against the hatch and rested her head between them.

Then she remembered her task wasn't over yet—far from it. She ran to the other end of the airlock and opened the portal to the *Duchess*.

"We're in," she said to her troops. "Search and secure the ship in your allotted fire teams."

The atmosphere in the mercs' vessel had flooded the *Bathsheba's* airlock when the ships had first connected. The airlock sensors would detect the existing air pressure, and—

A *thunk* behind her signaled a hatch opening.

She swung around. The hatch slid to one side and she got her first view of the interior of the inter-sector ship.

All was dark inside the *Bathsheba*, though the light cast from the *Duchess* and the mercs' helmets reflected from shiny metallic surfaces within. Through the figures of soldiers pouring into the ship, Carina also thought she could make out contoured glass structures.

A brilliant flash in the darkness suddenly revealed the *Bathsheba's* innards in stark relief, like lightning illuminating a landscape.

But she had no time to process what she saw inside the ship.

The flash had been a pulse round.

The Black Dogs were under attack.

7

Mercs were running into the other ship. Parthenia's guess had been correct: the *Duchess's* docking port was open and glimpses of another vessel were visible through it, between the figures of the soldiers.

A battle was going on.

She'd seen enough fighting over the previous few months to recognize the intermittent flashes of pulse fire, and her helmet's audio was picking up its signature hiss and fizz.

The battle seemed to have only just started. Black Dogs were still pouring through the portal.

She ran to the end of a line of soldiers waiting to join the battle, hoping she wouldn't be noticed and ordered to return to her cabin. The man she stood behind turned around and glanced at her, but if he realized she wasn't one of the regular mercs he didn't say or do anything about it.

The front of the line jerked into action, and seconds later the movement reached the end of the line. Parthenia found herself jogging into the darkness of the other ship. Her visor's night vision activated, and she was surrounded by a confusing scene of moving ghostly figures and bursts of light.

Her group took up a position at the rear of the fight, only a little way beyond the entrance to the new ship. Perhaps they were waiting for further orders.

She stuck close to the soldier who had been at the end of the line, while she tried to figure out what was going on and how she could help.

Parthenia reminded herself she would have to be careful not to mistakenly Cast at someone on her own side. The Black Dogs' HUDs would show the status of any soldier that came into view—whether they were friendly or an enemy—but her suit was not connected to the battle comm system and her visor didn't have that capability.

The pulse fire intensified, and in the increased light she began to make some sense of her surroundings.

The enemy ship was *huge*. She hadn't noticed until the new illumination revealed it, but the ceiling hung tens of meters overhead. The fighting seemed to be taking place in a chamber equally as wide, though it was hard to be sure. Pulse fire was reflecting from the walls, along with the figures of soldiers, making it difficult to judge distances.

She shifted her position slightly to give herself a better view. The oval, glass coverings of a thousand or more receptacles protruded from the walls and rose in ranks almost to the ceiling. A walkway ran in front of each row above floor level. Square patches of darkness below the first walkway suggested exits to the large chamber.

She was no expert on starships, but this didn't look anything like her expectation of a destroyer, which could only mean they were aboard the inter-sector ship!

From what she could tell, the Black Dogs were trying to reach the exits and, presumably, get deeper into the ship, and the enemy was trying to stop them.

She could definitely lend her side a hand.

Parthenia sucked elixir through the tube in her suit and

Cast Enthrall on the nearest soldier she was confident wasn't a
Black Dog. The man stopped firing. His arms relaxed and his
weapon hung loose in his hands.

She took another drink of elixir and focused on his neighbor, but before she could Cast, her new target noticed the
Enthralled soldier. He nudged him with his elbow, and the man
raised his rifle and began firing again.

Dammit!

That was the problem with Enthrall: the person affected
would obey whatever command they were given. The neighbor
must have comm'd the first soldier and told him to shoot. *Who*
he would fire at was unpredictable but he was essentially back
in action.

Her next option was to Transport the enemy, but she wasn't
sure where to Transport them to. She could either put them
into space or elsewhere on the inter-sector ship. If she put them
into space they might not survive until they were picked up—
they were wearing armor, not EVA suits. Though she wanted to
help, she quailed at the idea of actually killing someone. And
Transporting them elsewhere on the ship would mean creating
a threat lying in wait for the Black Dogs as they moved
through it.

As Parthenia was trying to figure out what to do, more
enemy soldiers arrived, racing into the chamber through the
right-hand entrance. The pulse fire escalated as the mercs tried
to push forward. The atmosphere was bright with constant
flashes, but, save for the soft buzz of rounds and the movements of the soldiers, it was oddly quiet. All commands and
cries of those hit were confined behind the dark visors of the
soldiers' helmets.

Yet more of the enemy arrived. The mercs were becoming
outnumbered. Despite their best efforts, they started to fall.

The front line was being forced back.

If the Black Dogs didn't gain control of the ship, their plan would fail. They would have to remain in the sector where the Dirksens wanted their blood. Carina would have to abandon her dream of traveling to Earth. Worse, the enemy soldiers could push all the way into the *Duchess* and take the mercs' ship. That would be a disaster.

She had to do something.

She had an idea.

The Cast was one she'd rarely practiced, let alone used, but she knew the Character. And if her idea didn't work, she didn't *think* it would cause any harm.

The problem was timing. The damned lag meant she would have to Cast randomly and hope for the best.

She closed her eyes, wrote the Character in her mind, and sent it out.

She opened her eyes.

Nothing seemed to happen.

Disappointment and fear settled on her. She'd thought the Cast would have *some* effect at least, not nothing at all. And in the short time it had taken her to perform it, more mercs had fallen and the enemy had edged closer.

Then it hit her: she'd waited so long after swallowing elixir that it had probably lost its efficacy.

There was no way to find out except try again.

Brilliant light burst in her vision, and the man she was sheltering near fell sideways onto her. She grunted as his heavy figure impacted her small frame. He'd been hit by a stray pulse round that had made it through to the back line. She pushed him with her shoulder and he managed to straighten up, moving off her.

Parthenia sucked up a mouthful of elixir and swallowed it.

Again, she wrote the Character. Again, she sent it out in the direction of a section of enemy fire.

As she opened her eyes, the Cast hit.

Almost too fast to see, the pulses flashing from the enemy's rifles hit an invisible barrier. Some appeared to disintegrate and scatter. Others bounced off it.

She'd done it! She'd only known that Repulse could deflect Casts. The idea that it could be used against pulse rounds had been a pure guess, but it had actually worked.

Some rounds had even rebounded at the enemy soldiers. They stopped firing and seemed confused, turning their heads toward each other as if checking they'd all noticed the same thing.

The Black Dogs who had been targeting that section seemed similarly nonplussed. Their firing slackened along with that of their antagonists, but the brief lull was soon over.

Parthenia surveyed the battle, trying to discern the spot where the Black Dogs were pressed the hardest. When she found it, she took a drink of elixir, and then closed her eyes.

She was in the middle of writing the Repulse Character when someone roughly shook her shoulder, startling her.

The Character faded, half-drawn, and she opened her eyes to see a soldier facing her.

"Parthenia," came Carina's voice over her comm, "I guessed it might be you who pulled that stunt. Did you Repulse those rounds?"

"Yes, I did," she replied proudly.

"What the hell are you doing here? Get back to the ship."

"Huh? No! I'm staying here. I want to help."

"It's far too dangerous," Carina snapped. "This is a *battle*, for stars' sake. You could be killed. Go back to our cabin and stay there. That's an order."

"You can't tell me what to do—"

"Just watch me. This isn't the place for an argument. If you don't go right now, I'll order Halliday here to pick you up and *carry* you back, and that'll take a valuable soldier away from the battle."

Parthenia noted her older sister wasn't threatening to

Enthrall her, as she'd done in the past, but she seemed determined to make her leave, despite the fact Parthenia had clearly demonstrated her worth.

"*I'm* valuable," she protested, anger building. She was too old to be bossed about, especially by someone only a few years older than her. "You wanted us with you on Ostillon, when—"

"Leave!" Carina yelled. "Now!"

Parthenia was furious. How dare Carina speak to her like that?

But if she knew anything about her sister, once she'd set her mind on something she would follow through, no matter what. If she didn't go, Carina really would tell someone to manhandle her out of the place, and that would be humiliating beyond belief.

"I *hate* you!" she exclaimed. "I hate you, and the first chance I get I'm leaving. I'll go so far away I'll never have to see your face again!"

She turned and stalked out of the chamber.

8

Carina watched her sister until she disappeared into the *Bathsheba's* airlock.

Idiot! Why couldn't she understand this was no place for a sixteen year old?

When she'd first noticed the weird behavior of the pulse rounds, she'd been as confused and amazed as everyone else. It was only when it occurred to her the pulses appeared to rebound from an unseen barrier that she put two and two together and realized they'd been Repulsed. And as she hadn't made the Cast, it had to be one of her siblings.

After that, it hadn't been hard to spot Parthenia's small figure crouched behind Halliday.

It was a relief that her sister finally left the firefight, but Carina couldn't deny her idea about using Repulse against weapon fire was brilliant. She hadn't imagined it could be used in any other way than to deflect attacking Casts.

Now, with Parthenia's trick up her sleeve, she might be able to turn the tide of the battle.

She returned her attention to the fight. In the brief time it had taken to dismiss her sister, the mercs had lost more ground.

Some were wounded and either crawling away from the fighting or being dragged from it by their buddies. A few were motionless and beyond reach.

Yet more soldiers sent by Lomang's wife were running into the chamber from all its entrances. The woman appeared to be concentrating all her forces on this spot, and it was working: she had them pinned down, but not for long.

Carina comm'd every merc she'd kept back in reserve, sending them all forward into the fight. At the same time, she began to Cast.

Taking large swallows of elixir, she Repulsed one section of enemy weapon fire after another. She found that, after a few tries, she could finesse the angle of the Casts so the pulses flew straight back at their originators. Their antagonists were being hit by their own rounds as well as the mercs', and they began to fall.

Worse than the onslaught of their own firepower was the confusion and dismay the phenomenon sowed among the troops. As each Cast took effect, the fighters targeted briefly stopped firing as they tried to make sense of what was happening. Then, probably urged by their CO, some resumed their attack, but others appeared to be too shaken to continue or too fearful of their own fire returning to them.

Slowly at first, but then with increasing speed, the mercs began to gain ground. They reached the fallen comrades they'd been forced to abandon and were able to retrieve them while the majority of their force pushed forward.

Carina remained at the rear as she had to concentrate on Casting, which left her vulnerable to attack. But, along with the Black Dogs, she was also able to move out into the chamber. The enemy troops were retreating toward the entrances, leaving behind the incapacitated among them.

She was pleased at the sight of the fallen enemy. If any survived, they would be useful sources of intel.

"Car," came Atoi's voice through her comm. "Sitrep."

She gave the situation report succinctly, not wanting to waste time talking when she still had Casting to do.

"Great," Atoi replied. "Cadwallader had me guarding the airlock, but it looks like most of the destroyer's forces have been deployed aboard the *Bathsheba*. I'm coming over. ETA four minutes."

The news was welcome. More mercs would be needed for mopping up.

Carina sucked on the tube in her suit for more elixir, but nothing came out. She'd used up her supply.

Shit.

She needed a bigger reservoir—an inexhaustible one, preferably.

But it was clear the mercs had the advantage now anyway. Her Casts were no longer crucial to deciding the battle. From the look of things, it would only be a matter of moments until—

Suddenly, their adversaries broke ranks and ran for the exits.

That was it. Lomang's wife had ordered a retreat.

Carina gave commands to her troops to chase down the enemy.

Though she was loath to leave her troops during this crucial part of the mission, she decided to return to the *Duchess* to replenish her supply of elixir. Her ability to Cast could be vital in the clean up operation.

Wounded mercs were lying within the *Bathsheba* and beyond it on the other side of the *Duchess's* docking port. That was no surprise, but she realized with a jolt that the small figure moving among them was Parthenia. Her sister hadn't gone back to their cabin as ordered. She'd stayed behind to Heal the injured troops.

Carina didn't feel she had any right to criticize the girl for her decision. As she stepped quickly past her, she squeezed her shoulder through her armor.

Then she raced to the galley, where a tank of elixir was stored.

As soon as she'd refilled her suit's supply, she dashed to the shared cabin.

"Jace!" she exclaimed as she saw the mage sitting with her siblings. Before he could answer, however, she said, "Could you go to the docking port and help Heal the wounded? Parthenia is already there."

"Of course," he replied, rising to his feet.

"We'll go too," said Oriana. "Me and Ferne. Right, Ferne?"

"No," Carina said firmly. "It's still dangerous there. We only just drove out the soldiers from the destroyer. I want you to stay here with Darius and Nahla."

"But—"

"No!" she yelled, making the children jump.

Even Jace looked taken aback. But he said gently, "Do what your sister says, kids."

Carina left the cabin and ran back in the direction of the *Bathsheba*, leaving Jace to follow at his own pace. She'd already been absent from the fight for several minutes.

Cadwallader comm'd, asking for an update. She filled him in as she ran.

"Good," he said when she'd finished. "I'm going to join you."

When she arrived at the chamber in the inter-sector ship, Atoi and ten other mercs, including Bryce, were already there.

"It's almost ours, but not quite," she told them. "We're rooting out the clingers-on. Rather than retreating to their destroyer, they might try to make a stand somewhere and push us back."

"It's a damned big ship," said Atoi, looking upward at the

rows of oval, transparent-fronted cubicles that ran around the walls.

"Yeah," Carina agreed. "It's going to take hours to search it."

Cadwallader strode in, armored up. "I'm taking over from here. Atoi, half of your team is to accompany Lin to search the top level. Take the remaining half with you to search the engine service tunnels."

Atoi's dark visor hid her features, but Carina could easily imagine the face her friend must have pulled on hearing she'd been given the worst job. Investigating the narrow passages engineers used for physical access to the ship's engines would be extremely taxing and dangerous. Yet the lieutenant colonel was right to give his most senior, capable, and experienced officer the job. If Lomang's wife wanted to hit them where it hurt, she would sabotage the *Bathsheba's* engines.

"Yes, sir," Atoi replied, with only a trace of resentment.

She quickly named the mercs who were to accompany Carina.

Bryce was among them.

"Sir," Carina said to Cadwallader, "don't forget about the booby traps."

"I haven't forgotten," he replied dryly.

She led her soldiers toward the nearest exit, unsure how to get to the highest level. She guessed there had to be elevators, though the inter-sector ship wasn't like anything she'd ever encountered.

9

Outside the chamber, beyond the light that spilled through from the *Duchess*, all was dark. A suggestion to activate her helmet light appeared on Carina's HUD but she ignored it and told the others to do the same. They could operate on night vision without any great disadvantage and there was no point in advertising their presence to the enemy.

She halted. The wall directly in front of her bore the signs of a firefight. Scorch marks and melted patches revealed that the Black Dogs pursuing their antagonists had met with some resistance. But the fight was over and the passage was empty.

She was about to move on after a cursory look at the damage when something drew her attention. Leaning closer, she peered at one of the scorched areas.

"Hey," she comm'd her team, "take a look at this and tell me if I'm imagining it."

As she moved aside, Bryce and another man, Gulay, stepped over to see what she meant.

"Stars," breathed Gulay. "How is it doing that?"

So she wasn't going crazy. The mark really was fading at a

rapid pace. The melted area was quickly returning to its original state.

"It's repairing itself," said Bryce. "I've never seen that before. Is that unusual?"

She sometimes forgot that he'd only spent time aboard starships since getting mixed up with her. "As far as I know, it's unheard of."

The three other soldiers in the team also examined the blemished surfaces, running their gloved hands over the wall as it changed.

"Okay, let's go," Carina ordered.

There would be time to discover the *Bathsheba's* interesting features later on, once the ship was secure. Plenty of time. They had a long journey ahead.

She walked quickly along the passage, looking for an elevator or another way to reach the top level. She hadn't gone more than a few meters when the atmosphere readings in her HUD began to alter, revealing the tell-tale signs of a firefight ahead. She comm'd Cadwallader, telling him about the resistance the Black Dogs had met.

"We're already on it," Cadwallader replied. "Continue as ordered, but avoid the engagement."

She reversed direction to lead her team away from the fight.

By the time they passed the site of the earlier battle again, the walls were entirely free of damage.

The passage began to curve and slope downward—another feature Carina had never encountered aboard a space vessel. She'd only ever known perfectly horizontal and vertical surfaces, but this slope was like the side of a low hill.

They rounded the curve, and the walls splayed out. In the center of the wider space a tube rose from the floor and disappeared through the ceiling. Double doors opened in the side as they approached.

Assuming it was an elevator, she ordered her team inside,

and the men and women crowded in. Six soldiers in full armor and bearing weapons were about all the available space would hold.

The doors closed.

She was relieved to see the elevator operated via buttons on a panel. If it had required voice commands in the strange language she'd seen on the display in the airlock, they would never get it to work.

She pressed the button for the seventh, uppermost level.

A few beats later, the doors opened into darkness.

"I wish someone would figure out how to turn on the lights around here," Bryce muttered.

They were in a place almost identical to the one they'd just left except it didn't slope and the elevator sat at a fork in the passage, offering three potential avenues for exploration.

How big was this level? If it spanned the entire ship it would take them hours to search it.

"We'll continue in pairs," said Carina. "If you see any signs of the adversary, comm me. Don't approach them until backup arrives. And," she added, recalling her own warning to Cadwallader about booby traps, "don't try to open or activate anything if it doesn't happen automatically."

Simply walking around inside the ship *could* set something off, but Lomang hadn't mentioned anything like that, and making sure none of the enemy remained aboard took priority.

She split up her team and assigned two pairs a passage each to explore before she realized the only people remaining without a partner were Bryce and herself.

"We'll take this one," she said uncomfortably.

She set off down the remaining passage, Bryce trailing a step behind.

The first door they encountered opened as they approached, revealing a storeroom holding stacks of folded textiles and large printer. After quickly checking around the

shelves, they moved on. The next room was also used for storage, though this one held electronics: mostly interfaces and
comm devices.

Carina was mildly bemused. The rooms were not secured
in any way, so it was clear that the ship's passengers were free to
take whatever they wanted from them. It was yet another
phenomenon she hadn't encountered before on a commercial
or military ship. The *Bathsheba* was more like a vast but
privately owned vessel.

At the next door, a security panel on the wall indicated it
would not be so easy to enter. The door didn't open as they
drew close to it.

"Does it require a code, maybe?" asked Bryce.

"Maybe."

But Lomang hadn't mentioned anything about codes to be
used inside the ship.

The panel's screen was a flat, black enigma.

"Looks like we won't be going in there," said Bryce.

She was reluctant to risk triggering a trap too, but she'd
spotted something.

She squatted down and peered at the line between the
bottom of the door and the floor. Reaching out, she pushed her
hand against the line, and then she realized she was right—a
tiny bit of light was spilling out from the rest of the gap, made
more obvious when she'd blocked out a section.

Whatever lay on the other side of the door, the lights were
on in there, which meant someone was inside.

"Shit," Bryce said, also staring at the light.

"I'm going to Open it," said Carina.

"How?"

She clicked her tongue against her teeth. "I'm going to
Open it."

"Oh." He took a few steps back and raised his pulse rifle.

She moved to one side, sipped elixir, closed her eyes, and Cast.

As she waited for the result, she tensed.

The door slid open smoothly.

She exhaled and peered through the doorway.

In the space that was revealed to them, the lights were not on. Not any artificial lights, at least.

A high dome overhung a wide interior. The dome was transparent, and beyond it was...space.

Military starships and even many commercial vessels rarely featured windows. They were a weak spot in a ship's hull and therefore an unnecessary risk during battles, and most transportation companies deemed them a needless expense. As a consequence, space travel generally allowed passengers few opportunities to look at the view. During Carina's days as a merc, she'd only seen the stars occasionally, when she happened to be planetside during an assignment.

Here, within the inter-sector ship, starlight bathed the room, glistening on every surface. A thick, shimmering band comprised of millions of brilliant specks set like tiny jewels in rich, inky velvet gleamed from above.

Carina exhaled deeply and walked through the doorway.

"Whoa," breathed Bryce as he joined her.

Then someone shot him.

ll Carina saw was the flash of a pulse round and, from the corner of her eye, Bryce toppling to the floor.

"NO!" she yelled, and dove down beside him.

Another flash flew over her head as she dropped.

Crouching, she lifted her rifle and returned fire.

"Bryce!" she comm'd. "Bryce! Can you hear me?"

A second offensive pulse flew out but missed them both. She glimpsed someone ducking behind cover.

She heard no reply from Bryce, but he rolled onto his side. The pulse had hit his left shoulder and chest. He reached feebly for his weapon, which had fallen from his hands, but there was no question he was out of the game, perhaps dying.

She had to make a decision lightning fast: Heal Bryce or fight off their attackers?

Before she even knew what she chose, she was hammering out shots. Then she was up and running, zigzagging randomly in the direction of the enemy. There had been no real choice to make—in the time it would have taken to Cast Heal on Bryce they would both be dead.

A pulse hit her visor, taking out her HUD and turning the shield opaque. She ran into something, a sharp edge ramming into her calf, and she spun head over heels, her back slamming into the deck.

She opened her visor. The cold ship's atmosphere rushed in, and the starlight dazzled her.

Her fall had winded her. As she sucked in air in a whoop, a dark figure loomed, black against the stars.

Though she'd fallen, she'd maintained a firm grip on her weapon. She raised it in one hand and shot the soldier square in the stomach. He slumped to his knees, clutching his midriff. Carina pushed the muzzle of her gun against his helmet and was about to fire when a voice called out,

"Stop! Don't kill him!"

The soldier entirely collapsed and sprawled on the floor face downward.

Moving her rifle so that the muzzle remained in contact with the wounded soldier's helmet, she sought out the voice's owner.

A small woman in armor emerged from behind a reclined seat and stepped toward her, empty hands raised.

"In front of me," Carina ordered as the woman reached her, transferring the muzzle from the man's head to her back.

She drove her captive forward quickly, guiding her over to Bryce.

He was still breathing, she saw with relief.

"Stop," she commanded.

Taking a drink of elixir, she knelt down, maintaining the pressure of her gun against the woman's back. After closing her eyes, and placing her hand on Bryce's wound, she Cast Heal.

As she opened her eyes, she noticed the prisoner peering over her shoulder. Carina jabbed the gun against her kidneys. "Eyes forward!"

After a pause, the woman obeyed.

"Bryce," she comm'd. "Are you okay?"

"Uh..." He moved the arm of the shoulder that had taken the hit. "Yeah. Thanks."

He sat up. "Suit's lost atmosphere, though." His visor opened, and he looked up at the woman. "Who's that?"

Carina was wondering the same. Her captive was very small for a soldier, which implied she wasn't a soldier at all.

"That thing you did..." said the woman, facing the darkness "...can you do it for my man as well?"

Carina glanced at the soldier she'd shot. He hadn't changed position.

"Why would I do that?"

"To save his life, of course."

"That doesn't answer my question."

Bryce had stood up. "Carina, maybe you should..."

"You remember he nearly killed you, right?" she asked acidly.

"He's just a man doing his j—"

"You don't know that."

"While *she's* clearly something else," Bryce finished.

Carina had formed the same opinion, and she had a good idea of what kind of *something else* the woman was.

She sighed. "Okay," she grumbled. "*If* he's still alive. Cover her."

Leaving Bryce guarding their captive, she returned to the stricken man. With some effort, she rolled his bulky form over. He didn't make a sound but his arms and legs moved a little. The close-range pulse round had done its work. Gray-blue guts gleamed wetly through burned gaps in his armor.

Swallowing bile, she turned her face away and sipped elixir.

Moments later, after sending out the Heal Cast, she looked back at the soldier. New, pink skin had grown over his intestines, though they were still faintly visible. He would live, though he would probably need time to fully recover.

"Get up," she ordered.

He squirmed, appearing to make an effort to stand.

"Come on," she urged, "or I'll change my mind about allowing you to live."

The soldier's movements became more urgent. He struggled to his feet.

"Over there," said Carina, "with your commander."

Weaving as he walked and with both hands clutching his stomach, the man made his way toward the woman and Bryce. In the half-light of the starscape, the two were shadowy shapes in the darkness.

There was no doubt in her mind that the woman was Lomang's wife. She didn't look, move, or act like a soldier, and she'd referred to her companion as 'my man', so she was clearly his superior.

As Carina approached them, she comm'd Cadwallader. "I've picked up two of the enemy." She didn't want to let on to the woman that she knew who she was.

Let her sweat a while.

"Where should I take them?"

"Where are you?" the lieutenant colonel asked.

"In some kind of viewing dome."

"Right. So, it's just two of them? What were they doing in there?"

Shit.

Cadwallader had made a good point. What *had* Lomang's wife and her companion been doing in the dome? It was only by chance that she and Bryce had found them. Had they been hiding? That didn't make any sense—they would have been cut off from the rest of the company from the destroyer, and eventually they would have been found.

And it was hardly the time or place for a romantic assignation.

The enemy soldier had reached Lomang's wife and Bryce. He was managing to stand, but he was hunched over.

"Take off your helmets, both of you," Carina ordered. She didn't want them to be able to comm each other.

They complied, though the man moved slowly.

The woman's hair was thick, black, long, and wild. She brushed it away from her small, delicately featured face, and regarded Carina narrowly with dark eyes.

The man looked similar to the men in Lomang's crew she'd seen aboard the *Zenobia*: he was wide-mouthed, his head was large and bony, and his beard was carefully styled.

"Why are you here?" she asked. "What were you doing?"

Lomang's wife's eyes narrowed further and she tossed her head haughtily, flinging her long hair over her shoulder.

The man only looked down.

Carina clenched her jaw. "Look, I don't have time for a conversation. You know how I Healed your man? Well, I can do other stuff too. In the blink of an eye I can move you from where you're standing to out there." She pointed to the starry expanse beyond the dome. "And we can all watch you die."

The woman remained silent, but she began to look doubtful.

"She can do it," said Bryce, "and she has."

Two tense beats passed, then Lomang's wife said, "I've heard something of your powers. At first, I thought the report was only the babbling of a fool, but then I saw what you did to him." Her gaze flicked to Bryce. She breathed in deeply, and then exhaled. "I believe you."

She continued, "If you look over there you will find an explosive device." She indicated a spot on the other side of the room. "I planned on blowing a hole in the hull, in here where it's weakest. In the resulting confusion and distraction, my forces would be able to retake the ship."

Carina's chest tightened. "Is the device about to go off?"

The woman's eyes flashed and her nostrils flared, as if she were barely keeping her emotions in check.

"Answer!" Carina pushed the barrel of her rifle into the woman's chest, causing her to stagger backwards.

"No," she muttered. "I hadn't set it when you came in."

"Bryce," said Carina, "go and find the explosives and check they aren't dangerous, but be careful. I'll watch these two."

In spite of her natural enmity toward Lomang's wife, Carina felt a modicum of respect. The woman's plan could have worked, and it was something she herself might have done in similar circumstances.

"What's your name?" she asked her.

Lomang's wife drew herself up to her full height, which was about the level of Carina's shoulder. "I am Mezban Kabasli Noran, Procurator of the Majestic Isles, Member of the Encircling Council, and *your* nemesis."

11

A board the *Duchess*, all was chaos. Mercs pounded the corridors, and the same acrid gases of battle Carina had perceived on the *Bathsheba* permeated the atmosphere.

She'd sent Bryce to the sick bay to get checked out, reluctantly allowing the enemy soldier to go with him. Mezban Kabasli Noran was on her way to the brig, Carina's gun at her back, though navigating the ship through the racing mercs was proving difficult.

Cadwallader and Atoi weren't answering her comms, and she didn't want to stop anyone to ask what was going on. There seemed to be fighting somewhere aboard the ship, which was odd. She'd thought the main battle was over. Maybe the Black Dogs had captured some enemy soldiers and they'd broken out of confinement.

She hadn't decided whether to put Mezban in the same cell as her husband, but it looked as though the question might have been decided for her. If some of the woman's soldiers were also to be held in the small brig, Lomang and his wife might have to be reunited, whatever the consequences.

Judging from Mezban's previous behavior toward her husband—forcing him into a tiny shuttle and ejecting him from his ship—the consequences for the smuggler would be dire.

Yet when Carina arrived at the brig, its only occupants were Lomang, Pappu, and Calvaley.

The reactions of the smuggler and his twin were something to behold: Lomang's eyes widened until his irises were islands in a white ocean, and his mouth fell open so far he seemed about to dislocate his jaw.

Pappu, on the other hand, looked the most frightened she'd ever seen him, and possibly the most frightened she'd ever seen anyone. He darted to the rear of his cell and spreadeagled himself against the wall, facing Mezban with features full of terror.

Carina became seriously concerned the gigantic man might wet himself.

"Not in this cell!" he pleaded. "I beg you. Not in here. Put her in with the old man, or take me out!"

By contrast, Lomang flung himself at the transparent cell wall and pressed his face against it, flattening his nose and smashing his lips until they were flat, pink pancakes.

He moved his head away just long enough to say, "My love! My sweetest darling! We're together again at last." Then he squashed his face against the surface again, as if trying to push through the solid barrier to reach her.

Mezban murmured something indistinct. She continued to talk, her voice becoming louder, and Carina realized she was speaking the foreign language the smuggler had used to speak to his men. She spoke louder and faster, and her face began to twist with fury. The woman's delicate olive skin flushed deep red, her eyes grew fiery, and as she—apparently—cursed and scolded Lomang, spit flew from her lips.

Her tone rose to a crescendo, and she tried to wrench her

arm from Carina's grip, raising it in a gesture of fury. She struggled to break free and when that failed, she attempted to drag Carina toward the smuggler's cell.

Lomang's eyes shone as he watched her, his face wreathed in admiration and, Carina noticed with disgust, what looked like lust.

She curled her lip. The display from the married couple was both hilarious and disturbing.

"I think you'd better go in here," she said, hauling the furious woman over to Calvaley's cell.

The old man looked up in alarm as he understood what was happening.

"No, no," he said, standing up from his bunk, "I don't believe..."

She asked the guard to unlock the cell door, and then pushed Mezban inside.

As she walked away, the sound of Lomang and Mezban's voices, one conciliatory and adoring, the other impassioned and enraged, followed her down the corridor.

After a second failed attempt to comm Cadwallader and Atoi to find out what she should do next, she decided to pop in on the kids and check they were okay. She also wanted to make sure Parthenia had returned to their shared cabin too. She was worried her sister might have gone to fight in the skirmish that seemed to be going on.

But when she arrived at the cabin, it was empty.

She stood in the entrance, taking in the vacant bunks and discarded clothing.

Her pulse began to race. Where had they gone?

She comm'd Bryce.

"Hey, are the kids with you?"

"No, it's just me and—"

"Do you know where they are?"

"No, sorry. Have they—"

She closed the comm.

Her mind was spinning.

The situation aboard the *Bathsheba* remained dangerous, and some kind of engagement was going on in the *Duchess*. If any of her brothers or sisters got tangled up in either operation they could be hurt or killed.

Dammit!

Her thoughts flew to Parthenia. The stupid girl had wandered into a full-on battle, had she dragged her siblings into something similar? If she had, Carina would never forgive her.

She stepped quickly to a bunk and picked up a pajama top. Holding onto the thin material, she took a drink of elixir and Cast Locate.

In her mind, the *Duchess* was a black, gray, and white landscape in a lifeless void. A single figure shone out among the many others moving around on the ship.

Nahla!

The clothes she was holding belonged to her youngest sister, but finding the girl didn't help her. If Carina Sent to non-mage Nahla, she wouldn't hear her.

Attempting to steady her panicked breathing, she grabbed another top. She was sure this one was Oriana's.

After swallowing more elixir, Carina tried the Cast for a second time.

Once more, she perceived the shadow of the *Duchess's* interior, like a splicer's scan of a person. Suddenly, Oriana gleamed out, clear and shining.

Thank the stars!

Now she could find out where the kids had gone and if they were all safe.

Before she had a chance to Cast Send, however, the cabin door flew open.

"Carina!" yelled Darius, rushing in and launching himself

into her arms. The force of the little boy almost knocked her over.

"You came back!" exclaimed Oriana. "What was the battle like?"

"Never mind that," said Ferne. "Tell her what we've been doing." Then, without giving his sister a chance to go along with his suggestion, he continued, "We had a battle of our own. We saved the ship!"

Carina sat very still. Darius's arms were around her neck and he was sitting on her lap, but she didn't move.

She could feel the blood draining from her face as her rage rose.

Oriana, Ferne, and Nahla gazed at her, their excited, triumphant expressions fading to dismay.

Darius's arms slipped away and he climbed off her before standing with his head hung low.

"What's wrong?" Ferne asked cautiously.

"Did I give you permission to leave the cabin?" asked Carina between her teeth.

Oriana replied, "No, but—"

"Did I tell you you could take part in a *firefight*, for stars' sake?"

"We had to!" Ferne protested. "The ship was being boarded at the airlock. If we hadn't—"

"He's right," said Oriana, her tone defiant. "And we helped. We really did. We Cast Lock, and we Transported some of the enemy soldiers, and—"

Carina leapt to her feet. "You could have been killed!" she yelled, her hands clenched at her sides. "You could all have died!"

"Jace was there too," said Ferne, his lip sticking out stubbornly. "He said it was okay for us to join in, as long as we stayed back."

"Jace *isn't* your family," Carina spat. "He doesn't have the right to give you permission to risk your lives. Stars!" She slammed her forehead with the palm of her hand. "Haven't you learned anything from the battle on Ostillon? Darius is lucky to be alive. It could all have gone horribly, horribly wrong."

"But you—"

"I know!" Carina roared. "I *know* I was the one who took you there! I know it was my fault Darius nearly died!"

She couldn't bear looking at the scared, confused faces of her siblings any longer. She stomped to the cabin door, pushing past Oriana and Ferne, and left.

12

T he soldier wasn't going to make it. Parthenia had exhausted her supply of elixir trying to Heal him, but his injuries were too severe. He'd been shot in the chest, arm, and thigh. It was the chest wound that seemed to be the problem. Receiving a pulse round in that area had done something to his heart that the Heal Cast couldn't fix.

Parthenia's throat tightened as she knelt next to the dying man, remembering Mother. When life could no longer be sustained and the end came, Heal only forestalled the inevitable. She'd tried over and over again to prevent her mother from slipping away, but all her efforts were useless.

She looked up, suddenly aware that she and the doomed merc were the only two people remaining in the *Bathsheba's* airlock. The fight inside the ship appeared to be over, and the soldiers she'd already helped had gone somewhere else, perhaps assigned new duties.

Should she tell the man there was no hope? She trembled at the thought of delivering such terrible news. Yet maybe he had some last messages or instructions to leave about things that were important to him. If only one of his fellow soldiers was around, or an officer, or even Carina—anyone else would be better suited to the task.

The man's visor opened. Parthenia sucked in a breath. Blood from his chest wound had splashed up onto his neck and face, which was also scorched red and blistered from the heat. His eyes were open and he was looking at her.

She tried to force a smile, but she feared she was only managing a grimace.

The soldier's mouth worked and his neck muscles tightened as he tried to speak. A few quiet words squeezed out. "Thanks... for trying."

Parthenia could see the life in his eyes begin to fade. Tears rose up, over spilled, and rolled down her cheeks.

"I'm sorry," she whispered. "I'm so sorry."

"Did..." the man swallowed "...what you could."

She took his hand in both of her own, determined to give him some comfort, at least.

"Hey, Scanlon," called a voice.

In her distraction, Parthenia hadn't noticed the thud of a merc's boots as he ran into the airlock.

"What are you doing there?" Without waiting for an answer, the new arrival went on, "Lazing around again, huh? Move out of the way, please, miss."

Somewhat dumbfounded by the merc's brusque, jokey manner, Parthenia moved aside.

"He's..." She wanted to convey the dying man's state to the other soldier, hoping to prevent his further suffering, but she couldn't find the words.

The soldier squatted down and scooped Scanlon into his arms. With a grunt of effort, he lifted the limp form, and then carried him away into the *Duchess*.

Parthenia was suddenly alone. She felt numb. How many soldiers had she Healed? She couldn't remember. They had come and gone so fast. She'd Healed some of them twice—they'd returned to the battle only to be wounded again.

A heavy blanket of exhaustion settled over her. She felt weak and faint, probably due to the large number of Casts she'd made in a short space of time. But it was more than that: it was the pain, the wounds, the groans and cries of the injured, that had done something to her. Witnessing so much suffering had left an imprint on her soul.

Slowly, she got to her feet. She guessed the Black Dogs must have won the battle with the soldiers from the destroyer. The vast, dark chamber beyond the *Bathsheba's* airlock was empty. Even the injured and dead enemy troops had disappeared. And no sounds were coming from within the *Duchess*.

It was time to return to her family and check they were okay.

Returning to the mercs' vessel and lighted areas, Parthenia lifted her visor. Distant shouts and thuds came to her from afar. It sounded like something was happening on the other side of the ship. Another fight, perhaps.

She should go there and help out, but she needed more elixir, and she no longer had a weapon. She didn't recall what had happened to it.

The mages' elixir was stored in the galley, and she decided to go there first. Picking up another rifle from somewhere, assuming she could find one, was probably pointless. She was most helpful to the mercs as a mage, not a fighter, though her recent experience had left her feeling hopeless. The idea of Healing men and women so they could go out and get hurt again, or even die, sickened her.

She walked along the passage, turned a corner and then another, but then she stopped. She looked around her, confused. She'd thought she'd been heading toward the galley, but she didn't recognize this part of the ship. She turned around and went back the way she'd come, hoping to return to her starting point and figure out where she'd gone wrong.

During their journey to the inter-sector vessel, Carina had discouraged her siblings from wandering about, telling them they should stick to their cabin, the mess, the galley, and the few other general-use areas. What exactly her older sister was worried about, she'd never explained. It wasn't like they could fall off the ship or be captured by one of their several enemies.

She'd humored Carina for the most part and echoed her warnings to her brothers and sisters, but she was getting tired of her oldest sibling's constant, overbearing bossiness. For a long time, she'd looked up to Carina and respected her, notwithstanding that time when she'd Enthralled her, but those days were over.

Parthenia halted again, once more confused by her surroundings. She felt dizzy and nauseated. Putting a hand to her head, she tried to figure out where she'd taken the wrong direction, but images of wounded soldiers flashed across her mind, muddling her thoughts.

She decided to continue on, hoping to end up in familiar territory, or maybe she would see someone she could ask for help.

The far-off sounds of battle had faded. She walked slowly on, turning down random passages for several minutes, until suddenly she found herself near the cabin she shared with her family. Her pace sped up in her relief at finding herself nearly 'home', and she hurried toward the door.

It opened, and her relief redoubled when she saw all four children safe inside, though Jace wasn't with them, which was a disappointment. He'd said he would look after them while she was gone.

An atmosphere of gloom and despondency hit her almost palpably. The glum faces of her siblings pivoted toward her as one.

"Stars," she said. "What's happened? Did we lose?"

"No," Oriana replied. "We won. It's all over. The Black Dogs fought the attackers all the way back to their ship and then seized it."

She went on to explain how the enemy had also tried to board the *Duchess* through one of the airlocks, and that the children and Jace had helped to repel the troops.

"Carina found out," said Ferne despondently. "Well, we told her, thinking she wouldn't mind too much, considering we weren't hurt at all and we'd done a great job."

"Oh." Parthenia sat down heavily on a bunk. "I see." After experiencing her sister's reaction earlier when *she'd* tried to help in a battle, she could imagine how the revelation had gone down.

Her siblings' hurt and sadness cut her deeply. Their sister must have given them a severe tongue-lashing.

"Don't worry," she said. "Carina isn't going to tyrannize us anymore. I'll make sure of it."

13

A pile of ancient documents sat in the center of the table in the mission room, between Carina, Cadwallader, and Jace. The writings, charts, and maps represented everything she'd worked for over the last months, perhaps even a year or longer—she'd lost track of the time that had passed since escaping from the Sherrerrs. They represented all her hopes and dreams of a safe, happy future for her family and herself.

And yet, when she looked at them, in place of the joy and relief she might have expected to feel was only hollow emptiness. The old, dry paper seemed to symbolize what was at the heart of her.

Someone coughed.

She looked up. Jace's gaze was upon her, serious and questioning.

"So, as I *said*..." Cadwallader was also watching her intently and clearly annoyed. Apparently, he was having to repeat himself "...we have some closely related decisions to make, and we must make them now, before we set off on our long journey.

Firstly, what do we do with Mezban and her troops? Secondly, what do we do with Lomang and his brother, and, thirdly, what do we do with Calvaley? Do we leave them all behind and face the fact they may try to follow us, or, in Calvaley's case, inform the Sherrerrs where we've gone, do we take them with us, or do we 'dispose' of them?" His nose wrinkled as he stated the third option.

Killing the prisoners would be a drastic and painful act, but it couldn't be denied it was the choice that made the most sense in terms of safety. If they did perform the executions, they would be secure in the knowledge that the former occupants of the destroyer would never escape and retake it.

Carina imagined the sight of hundreds of bodies floating in the void, frozen and bloody.

"I'm deeply opposed to murder," said Jace, "no matter what the circumstances, though I admit that it's going to be hard to keep so many men and women securely confined."

"What about you, Lin?" Cadwallader asked. "What's your opinion?"

"My opinion is, I don't know why *he's* even here," she said hotly, glaring at Jace.

"I've already explained," said Cadwallader in a calm tone, "I value Jace's input, and—"

"Well I don't!" She gritted her teeth and added, more evenly, "He took my brothers and sisters into a dangerous situation without my permission. He allowed *children* to risk their lives. Those are not the actions of someone who thinks straight or cares about consequences. He has nothing to offer here. If you value the outcome of this mission, I suggest you exclude this man from our discussions."

"No." Cadwallader appeared to try to pierce her with his ice-blue stare. "Jace's and the other mages' help in the attack at the airlock was invaluable. If they hadn't been there Mezban's troops might have taken the *Duchess*. Where would we all have been then, including your siblings? He did the right thing at the time. He also has considerable experience in a position of significant responsibility, and he demonstrates maturity and fair-mindedness."

"And I don't, I suppose?" Carina pushed her chair back and stood up. "You're forgetting it was me who found these papers here, it was me who paid for the repair and updating of the *Duchess*, and it was *me* who armed and equipped the Black Dogs. I have the *Bathsheba* now. I don't need either of you." She reached out to sweep the documents up into her arms.

Cadwallader laid a heavy hand on top of the pile.

"Sit down, Lin. Don't be a fool."

"Carina," said Jace, "I'm sorry for taking your brothers and sisters with me to help in the battle. I knew you would have forbidden it, and I should have told them to stay behind. But also, I knew they'd gone with you into the old mage fortress on Ostillon, so I thought…"

She looked down, a lead weight pressing on her heart.

"I want Jace here as a balance between you and me," said Cadwallader softly. "Three is a good number for making the best decisions. Please, sit down."

The unusual gentleness from the lieutenant colonel calmed her and brought a lump to her throat. She swallowed and resumed her seat.

"I don't think holding so many prisoners should be much of a problem," she said. "The chamber where we fought the first battle…did either of you take a good look at it?"

"I haven't been aboard the inter-sector ship yet," said Jace.

Cadwallader replied, "I had other things to think about."

"To be honest, I'm not sure I'm right," Carina said, "and even if I am, there's no guarantee the system would still function for so many, but I believe the *Bathsheba* used to be a colony ship. I think the room beyond the airlock is a Deep Sleep chamber, designed to hold hundreds of colonists."

Cadwallader folded his arms and leaned back in his chair. "So, we could put Mezban's soldiers into Deep Sleep capsules. That would be the perfect solution, though temporary. We couldn't keep them there forever."

"But we could hold the troops, Lomang and Pappu, Mezban and Calvaley, in Deep Sleep until we're so far from civilization there's no threat of them finding a way to come after us," said Carina.

"I guess we're talking about marooning all of them on a remote but habitable planet," Jace said. "I confess I'm not very happy with that plan either, but I could live with it."

"Good." The lieutenant colonel nodded. "Let's investigate that possibility. I'll tell the tech team to look into it." He reached into the documents and began to spread a few on the table. "We're confident we have all the information we need from these to plot a course for Earth?"

Carina eyed the yellow, aged sheets. In the weeks it had taken to travel to the *Bathsheba*, she had pored over them, taking in every detail. The Star Map she'd spent years memorizing had only ever been a test for those who were determined to return to Earth, the place that had been so dangerous for their kind. The papers included the true coordinates for the home planet, but the mages had also written pages and pages in a strange script the ship's computer could only partially translate. The information included their history, their home in the mountains, their fight to leave for the stars, the long expedition to freedom, and the earliest days of their settlement.

It had been an emotional and harrowing experience for her, reading about the struggles and persecution of her ancestors. The details she'd managed to understand had been disconcertingly familiar, and she'd begun to doubt the wisdom of her desire to go to a place that mages had fought so hard to leave. In the end, she'd felt she'd gone through so much to find the documents, and put everyone else through so much, it was too late to back out.

"Yes," she replied shortly to Cadwallader's questions. "I'm sure."

"Then let's move on to the next phase," Cadwallader said. "We familiarize ourselves with the new vessel, make safe and dismantle all of Lomang's traps, and prepare for our voyage."

"Right," said Carina. "So, we're done?"

"For now."

She rose to her feet again. "I have some business to attend to. Excuse me."

Feeling Cadwallader and Jace's eyes on her, knowing they were going to talk about her the minute she left the room, she walked out.

"Bryce?" she comm'd.

"Hey!" He sounded happy to hear from her. "What's up?"

"Where are you? I want to talk."

"That sounds ominous," he joked.

Carina was silent.

"Er...I'm attending to the bomb Mezban planted."

"I'll be there soon."

Someone had figured out how to turn on the lights at the viewing dome. Carina stopped after walking into that high-vaulted place and looked up. The starscape was dim, outshone by artificial beams.

Her mood settled a notch lower.

"Over here," Bryce called out, from the edge of the room.

He was with a woman—an explosives expert, Carina guessed. He'd probably directed her to the location of the device and then stuck around to help out.

That was so typical of him, always wanting to help, always sticking around.

She walked over. The nondescript shapes and lumps she'd seen on her first visit to the chamber turned out to be lamps, seats, tables, and loungers. The place was set up for socializing. A party under the stars would be quite something.

She passed a low table. Was this what she'd run blindly into after her visor was hit? Was that empty area beyond it where she'd landed and then shot Mezban's man in the stomach when he arrived to finish her off?

She walked on.

"Everything okay?" Bryce asked when she reached him.

"Not really."

The woman he was with looked between them. "I'm finished here. The bomb's disarmed. I'll take it and get out of your way." She lifted a device from the floor.

"Do you need a hand, Rosa?" asked Bryce.

"No, thanks. I can manage."

Carina stood in silence, looking down, waiting for the woman to leave. After hearing the door close, she went to speak.

"Wait," Bryce said, raising a hand. "Before you say anything, look at this."

He reached out to a sensor on the wall and swiped across it.

The lamps overhead blinked out.

Immediately, the stars shone down, brilliant, filling the space with ethereal light.

"Isn't it beautiful?" he asked. "It's different from looking at the night sky, right? The stars are brighter, and they're steady. They don't twinkle. There's something majestic about them, something sublime. Takes my breath away."

He moved behind Carina and wrapped his arms around her, hugging her tightly. Leaning down, he pressed the side of his face against her neck. "We should come back here sometime soon," he murmured. "Alone. When the kids have settled in."

He paused, and then went on, barely whispering, "We don't have to get married if you don't want to. I realized I was going too fast for you. I'd thought you were thinking the same as me, but I made a mistake. It's fine. I'll wait until you're ready, and if you're never ready, that's okay too."

She breathed in deeply. The feeling of his arms around her, his chest pressed against her back, and the soft bristles of his jaw crushed against her neck, was wonderful. She drank in his scent.

Gently, she took his arms and pulled them apart. She stepped away and turned around to face him. The starlight lit up his young features.

His expression broke her heart.

He'd guessed what was coming.

Touching his cheek, she said, "I can't do this. Not ever. I'm not the person you think I am. I'm not the person *I* thought I was. It wouldn't work, and I would hurt you. That's what I do."

She paused to press the edge of her sleeve against her eyes, stemming her tears.

"I'm so sorry. I'm sorry for dragging you all this way and making you a part of my fantasy. You've given up so much for me, risked so much, and I didn't deserve it. I didn't deserve *you.*"

She swallowed hard. "It's still not too late for you to leave. I can tell Cadwallader to make a detour to the nearest inhabited planet and I'll give you enough money to pay for your passage back to Ithiya. It'll take a year or longer to get home, I guess, but you'll make it eventually."

Bryce's gaze searched hers, his eyes shadow-black under the stars.

He leaned forward, took her face in his hands, and kissed her forehead. "I don't want to go back to Ithiya. I've gotten attached to your little family, Carina Lin. I'm coming with you to Earth."

She looked to one side, unable to meet his gaze.

Then she walked away, navigating the dark obstacles in the room carefully. When she reached the exit, she halted and turned. Bryce had sat down. Whether he was watching her or not, she couldn't tell.

She left him alone in the dark.

14

Three days later, Carina was helping to make the final preparations for their epic journey. Her misgivings about her plan to return to Earth had only grown since her meeting with Cadwallader and Jace, yet she had continued to not voice them. She felt as though the expedition was a boulder she'd levered, with great effort, from the top of a hill and now it was careering downward at a force and pace that was unstoppable.

She was putting the mage documents into a safe in a storage room aboard the *Bathsheba,* along with other precious items, carefully rolling up the brittle papers and tying thread around the scrolls before placing them inside the metal receptacle. She'd made copies of all the papers and stored the images on databases on the *Bathsheba* and the *Duchess*, which had been secured to the former vessel.

Mezban's destroyer, the *Peregrine*, had also been fixed to the inter-sector ship, and her troops were already in stasis. Carina hadn't been present at the time they had been made to go into the capsules, but she'd heard they'd been reluctant and fearful.

Somewhere out in the black was the ship they'd traveled in

from Geriel Sector, which held its own Deep Sleep facilities. Apparently, around three percent of the men and women Mezban had brought from her sector hadn't survived stasis. Whether the capsules on the other ship had been faulty or a three-percent failure rate in such systems was normal, Carina didn't know. However, it was no wonder the enemy troops had been afraid.

In a month or two, she would also be entering Deep Sleep. It was either that or live out years in space. But the report of the reaction of Mezban's soldiers had served to erode her convictions about the journey even further. If one of her siblings were to die in transit, she would never forgive herself.

She sighed and shook her head slightly as she tied the knot in a thread around the final document. After placing the scroll into the safe she closed it and set the lock. She wished she knew how to Cast a Lock that would last thousands of years and require detailed knowledge to Open, as the mages on Ostillon had, but the ability was beyond her. Perhaps Darius might be able to do it one day.

Though she'd had weeks to study the information the papers contained she still felt she'd only scratched the surface of it. Items like unfamiliar Characters and their related Casts, and details about the mages' mountain home on Earth had intrigued her but she hadn't been able to fully understand them.

She stood up and stretched her arms and back. There was still plenty more to do before their journey began.

As she relaxed and exhaled Parthenia walked in.

Her sister voiced a small *Oh!,* and halted. She turned, about to leave.

"Were you looking for something?" asked Carina.

"It's fine, it isn't important."

"Don't be silly. You obviously came here for something. What do you want?"

"It doesn't matter." Parthenia was almost out the door.

"For stars' sake, this is ridiculous!" Carina exclaimed. "Come back!" She marched over to her sister.

Parthenia halted. "What?" she spat. "What are you going to do? Grab me? *Force* me to stay and tell you why I'm here?"

Carina paused, taken aback by the girl's intense reaction. "No, I-I just think it's stupid for us to avoid each other."

"You aren't avoiding me, *I'm* avoiding *you*."

"Whatever. Look, I'm sorry for insisting that you left the battle in the Deep Sleep chamber, but it was for your own good." She reached out to touch her sister's arm, but Parthenia shrugged off the gesture.

"I care about you," said Carina, undeterred. She desperately wanted to put things right between them. "I know I have a strange way of showing it sometimes, but I do."

"That's right," said Parthenia. "You sure *do* have a strange way of showing it. But don't worry, I'm not going to let you 'care about me' any longer. And I've told the kids they don't have to mind you anymore. From now on, we're going to stick together and run our own lives." She poked Carina in the chest. "*You* can do whatever the hell you want."

She stalked away.

Carina's mouth dropped open. Suddenly, the coldness of her siblings toward her over the last few days made sense.

The day after the battle for the *Bathsheba*, Cadwallader had called another meeting to iron out the finer details of their forthcoming epic journey. Carina turned up a little early to the *Duchess's* mission room—the transfer of personnel and their effects to the *Bathsheba* had been due to begin the following day—and found the lieutenant colonel and Jace already there. The ancient mages' records remained on the table.

She nodded a greeting to them. "Right, where do we begin?" she asked as she sat down.

"We aren't starting yet," Cadwallader replied. "I took the

liberty of inviting some others along. I'd like to create a council of sorts. By my rough calculations we have twenty-four years of travel ahead of us, perhaps longer, through a largely unknown region of space. I want to bring together our best minds, and open out the decision-making process. We need to get our planning right, or perhaps suffer terrible consequences."

"Who?" Carina's gaze moved to Jace. Had he had some input into Cadwallader's decision? Why hadn't the lieutenant colonel asked *her* about this? "Who have you invited?"

As the words left her lips, Atoi walked through the doorway.

"Hey, Car," she said, raising a hand in greeting. "Hey, everyone. Thanks for the invite, sir."

She threw herself into a seat and reclined into its back, straightening out one of her long legs. "Who else is coming?"

"That's what I'd like to know," Carina muttered.

Voices could be heard chatting outside the room, drawing nearer.

Her heart fluttered in recognition.

Bryce and Parthenia entered.

Carina's lips drew to a thin line. She could understand Cadwallader's reasoning in including Bryce in the council, but Parthenia? She was a child. A smart, resourceful child, to be sure, but still a kid. Carina couldn't deny her sister had a valuable contribution to make, but how would she deal with the potentially disastrous fall-out from a decision she'd helped to make? Could she cope with the guilt and remorse when things didn't go to plan? The sleepless nights? The regret?

Parthenia was watching Carina as she sat down, a mixture of defiance and wariness on her face.

"We're all here," Cadwallader said. "Let's begin."

"Wait," said Carina.

The lieutenant colonel barely disguised a sigh. "Yes?"

"I'd like to know by whose authority you're 'opening out the decision-making process'? You certainly didn't speak to me about it." Her gaze turned to Jace. "Did he ask you?"

He coughed and looked uncomfortable. "No, but I agree with the principle."

"I don't understand what gives you the right to act unilaterally," Carina said tersely to Cadwallader.

He tapped his fingernails on the table. "We've been over this—"

"We have, and I *told* you I don't like you involving other people!"

"Look," said Bryce, "if my presence is going to be a problem, I'll leave."

"Me too," Atoi added. "To be honest, I hate sitting around talking, and I trust you guys to think up a good plan."

"This isn't about you two," Parthenia said. "It's about *me*. That's right, isn't it, sis?"

Carina doggedly maintained her focus on Cadwallader, but she saw her sister in her peripheral vision, glaring.

"You would prefer a more democratic process?" the lieutenant colonel asked in a tone dripping acid. "Very well. Jace has stated he agrees we should create a council to manage our journey to Earth, and I'm obviously of the same mind. You disagree. That makes it two against one. You're outvoted." He steepled his fingers. "Now we may continue."

Carina slammed the table with an open hand, making everyone jump. She felt like sweeping the documents off the table, upending it, and telling them all to get out.

But she fought her impulse to give further vent to her feelings, knowing she'd recently crossed the line with Parthenia for the second time. She said and did nothing else except clench her jaw.

After several moments of awkward silence, the lieutenant colonel said quietly, "Let's continue."

He pulled a piece of paper from the top of the pile and

passed it to Atoi, who was sitting nearest to him. "Assuming these are the true original galactic coordinates of Earth, as I said, we're looking at a journey of roughly twenty-four years and two months. Fortunately, we'll be spending most of the voyage in Deep Sleep. *Unfortunately*, despite the information from the mages, we aren't exactly sure where we're going. Though they recorded their time of departure from Earth, that doesn't seem to relate to current time measurements. They appear to have been using their local frame of temporal reference, not Standard Time. So, for our purposes, the date they give is useless, which makes adjusting our calculations to allow for the time that's passed since their departure difficult."

"I can tell you the number of mage generations born since leaving Earth, according to our lore," said Jace.

"You can?" Cadwallader's eyebrows lifted. "That may help."

Atoi passed the paper she was holding to Bryce.

"It's two hundred and forty-one," Jace said.

The lieutenant colonel's eyes moved up and left as he worked out the arithmetic. "That's well over seven thousand Standard years!"

Atoi whistled. "That's a heck of a long time to be away from home."

"I heard that human existence in this part of the galaxy is reckoned to date back about six and a half thousand years," Bryce said. "Jace's information fits in with mage history, which states they were the first human colonists of deep space."

"Interesting," said Cadwallader, "but a subject for another day. If mage lore is accurate, that means we can increase the reliability of our estimation of Earth's current location. Good. Now we need to hash out a rotation for individuals in stasis, among other things. How many should crew the ship while the rest sleep, and for how long?"

Bryce offered a suggestion, and then Jace offered another, and after a while the meeting had moved into a detailed discussion on the voyage. Carina didn't speak much, preferring to allow the others to make the decisions. Cadwallader had been a mastermind of organization, as always, and the people present mostly agreed with his proposals. She'd begun to see that he didn't really need their input; that his purpose in inviting the rest had been to make them feel included, that their opinion mattered.

Parthenia had made some intelligent, thoughtful contributions, and Carina felt proud of her, but whenever she'd tried to catch her sister's eye, Parthenia had purposefully ignored her.

It was no surprise that the girl was upset after their altercation at the battle, but as the discussion wore on, it had occurred to Carina that all her siblings had recently shown the same enmity. Ever since the taking of the *Bathsheba,* they'd been reserved and silent around her. Even little Darius had stopped climbing onto her lap.

Parthenia's announcement in the storage room, that her brothers and sisters were now going it alone without her input, made it clear to Carina that they'd decided to shun her.

She watched her sister walk away, the new understanding piercing her deeply. She'd pushed Bryce away, and now she'd lost her brothers and sisters too.

She heaved a deep sigh.

Parthenia turned a corner and disappeared.

Carina set her jaw.

She was alone again, but it was probably for the best.

15

"The rota's out!" said Ferne excitedly.

"It is?" Oriana jumped up from her seat and ran to him. "Show me!"

"Wait a minute," her brother replied, scanning the interface screen he was holding. "Let me look up our names."

Oriana pouted.

"Okaaay," drawled Ferne. "*You* can look us up." He handed her the screen.

His sister clutched it and squeezed in beside him on the armchair, pushing him aside with her butt.

Their two heads bent over the interface.

Parthenia had chosen a family suite on the *Bathsheba* for herself and her siblings. The habitation contained three bedrooms, and there had been some disagreement over who would sleep where. Oriana and Ferne had wanted to continue sharing a room, but Parthenia had pointed out that it might be better for the younger children to share with older siblings of the same sex.

The twins had agreed to her suggestion, though somewhat reluctantly, and now Ferne shared with Darius and Oriana shared with Nahla. The twins seemed to be getting along better as a consequence. They were certainly bickering less.

She'd taken the third bedroom for herself, where she slept in blissful solitude, with no one's feet poking in her face.

Family life since moving out of the *Duchess* and into the inter-sector vessel had generally been more peaceful. As well as having far more room to sleep, they also had the lounge where they were currently sitting, two bathrooms that they didn't have to share with less-than-hygienic soldiers, and access to printers that could create just about anything they wanted.

Not having Carina around anymore helped, too. Life was so much more pleasant without someone controlling your every move. It was true that their eldest sister—half-sister, Parthenia reminded herself—had helped them a lot in the early days, but those days were gone now. They were all older and much more experienced. They'd earned the right to be respected and trusted, but Carina hadn't or wouldn't accept it. They'd grown and matured in ways that their sister refused to acknowledge.

It was a shame that they'd been forced to push her out, but it had been inevitable, and there was only one person to blame.

"Does that rota thing say when we'll sleep and when we'll be awake?" asked Darius.

He'd found a printer that made paper and colored pencils, and he was busy drawing at the table. His efforts were heavily influenced by the hand-drawn pictures in the ancient mage documents: verdant mountains, high castles, stylized trees and flowers, and animal characters.

"Yeah, of course," Ferne replied. "It's the thing we've been talking about for *days*, remember?" he added in a tone that sounded as if he wanted to add *dummy* to the end of his sentence, but his gaze shifted to Parthenia and he stopped there.

Darius looked up at Nahla, who was sitting opposite him, also drawing, and rolled his eyes.

Nahla giggled.

"I've found our names!" blurted Oriana. "Let's see what we're doing." Her gaze tracked across the screen. When she registered what she was looking for, her mouth turned down at the corners. "Urgh, we're on the list of the first to remain awake." She looked more closely. "For eight months!"

"Yay!" said Nahla.

"No, not yay," Oriana said. "I want to go in a Deep Sleep capsule now and wake up when we get to Earth. Living aboard a starship is so *boring*."

"But we have a big ship to explore," said Nahla. "There's lots to do here, not like on the *Duchess*. Here, we can print stuff, go and look at the stars, play in the gym hall, explore the agri center..." She swung her legs as she chattered on about the things she and Darius had been doing since transferring onto the *Bathsheba*.

Everyone had been worried about Nahla after she'd witnessed the shuttle pilot's death on Ostillon and been trapped in the cabin with his dead body. She'd been withdrawn and quiet—crushed, almost—and the feeble light that had begun to glow in her since escaping their Dark Mage brother, Castiel's control, had been snuffed out. But, strangely enough, the cooling of relations with their eldest sister had made her louder and more assertive.

Nahla continued, "We can go anywhere we want now that Carina isn't around to..."

Her words dried up, and they all sat in unpleasant silence.

Darius appeared to be especially affected by the mention of his sister. He put down his pencil and looked as though he was about to cry.

He'd been the most reluctant to agree to separate from her. He hadn't said much in response to Parthenia's proposal, but his little face had spoken volumes as she explained what they needed to do and why.

In a way, it was ironic that he was the one who had resisted the idea—his heightened sensitivity to the emotions of those around him meant he was particularly vulnerable to Carina's regular bouts of anger. Yet perhaps it was to be expected. The two had always been close, ever since their sister had rescued him from the Dirksens.

A twinge of guilt hit Parthenia as she recalled the efforts Carina had gone to in protecting and helping them, but she pushed it away. Maybe the time would come when they could be one happy family again, but it was a long way distant. A big shift in attitude and behavior was required, and *not* on the part of the children of Stefan Sherrerr.

"Can I see the rota?" Parthenia asked, eager to move the subject on from their sister. She held out a hand to Oriana, who passed the interface over.

The information displayed reflected almost exactly what had been decided at the council meeting. Around three-quarters of the mercenaries were to go into Deep Sleep next week, but the rest would remain awake and on duty. The feeling had been that the *Bathsheba* was still at a small risk of attack and would remain so for several months, until she'd reached the vast galactic desert that lay before the Geriel Sector. Those who stayed awake during those months would be on hand to defend the ship. And, if necessary, the mercs in stasis could be brought out of it.

After the initial eight months of the journey were up, most of the remaining passengers would also enter the capsules. The small crew required to maintain the ship would be drawn from the pool of sleepers on a rotating basis, so that no one had to 'live' longer than three years on the ship in total.

At some point, when the *Bathsheba's* scanners detected a planet suitable for marooning Lomang, Mezban, and her troops, they would make a detour, but that was to be the only diversion in their journey to Earth.

During the part of the discussion when decisions were thrashed out about who would go into stasis, when, and for how long, Parthenia had argued that, firstly, the children would always be together, in stasis or out of it. The idea that one or two of them could grow older while the others slept was disturbing. Secondly, she'd insisted that the mages would be among those who would delay going into Deep Sleep until the ship was safe. Neither Carina nor Cadwallader had been able to deny that their powers were invaluable in a battle.

Knowing Oriana and Ferne might object to a delay before entering stasis, she hadn't said anything to them about what had been agreed upon, but they seemed to have accepted the fact fairly easily. They were already scrolling through sims the *Bathsheba* had available for the entertainment of passengers taking a break from stasis.

Parthenia checked the rota again. Bryce had elected to remain awake for the first eight months, too.

Yet she'd noticed that he and Carina didn't seem to spend any time together anymore. Carina had taken a single cabin, and she guessed Bryce had done the same. Something must have happened between the two of them and they'd split up.

The guilty twinge hit again.

She hadn't considered the impact that forcing her sister out of the family group would have on the man she'd come to think of as a brother. Rejecting Bryce as well hadn't been their intention. Did he think their decision extended to him? If he and Carina were no longer together, he might be uncertain about his relationship with them.

Putting down the interface, she decided to go and pay him a visit. She would let him know he was welcome to visit anytime —that they still liked him and wanted him in their lives.

As she stepped out of their suite into the corridor, however, she realized she didn't know where on the vast ship he was living. She connected to the ship's computer and asked for the location of his cabin. The answer took several seconds to arrive, which she took to mean the Black Dogs' techs were still struggling with integrating the *Duchess's* comm system with the *Bathsheba's*. Everyone was waiting for the person-to-person comm to come online.

Bryce had picked a place near the starscape dome Nahla had mentioned. Parthenia was still a little unfamiliar with the inter-sector ship's layout, but she knew the location of the viewing dome.

She set off, but she hadn't gone far before she spotted one of the mercenaries walking toward her with a determined gait. She avoided the man's gaze and moved to the side of the corridor to give him a wide berth, but he veered in the same direction.

She grew uneasy and annoyed. Was he going to try something, like that other soldier, Chandu? She'd been dismayed to hear the horrible man decided to remain with the Black Dogs after Carina had executed Sable Dirksen. He'd left her alone after she'd punched him, but she still didn't like the idea of sharing a ship with him.

Did this other merc have the same intentions?

The corridor was empty except for the two of them, she had no personal comm, and no one might hear her shout for help. Should she run back to her suite? She didn't want to look like a silly girl overreacting to the situation.

"Excuse me," said the merc as he arrived within talking distance. "It's Parthenia, right?"

"Yes, but, I'm sorry, I'm in a hurry."

"This won't take a minute."

Inwardly cringing, she halted.

The soldier looked very young for his profession. Parthenia guessed he must have joined up about the same age as Carina.

He held out his hand. "I wanted to say thanks—for saving my life."

"Oh! Uh…" She weakly shook his hand, realizing he had to be one of the mercs she'd Healed at the battle in the Deep Sleep chamber. "You're welcome," she said, excessively politely.

"You don't remember me, do you?" He was smiling. "My name's Scanlon, by the way. Kamil Scanlon."

The name rang a bell, but she still couldn't place him. "I'm sorry, but…"

"I guess I must have looked a lot different at the time. The doc rejuvenated my burned skin."

An image of a soldier opening his visor, revealing a seared face, covered in blood, and whispering his gratitude for her efforts to save him, popped into Parthenia's mind. "Stars!" she exclaimed. "I remember you now." She recalled another mercenary had scooped him up and carried him away. She'd been so sure he'd been beyond saving. "I thought you'd died!"

"Not yet," said Scanlon, with a wink. "But I might have if it hadn't been for you. You kept me alive until someone could get me to the sick bay. Even then, from what the medics said, it was touch and go. But I'm back to normal now, so I thought I would find you and show my gratitude."

"You don't have to do that. I was only doing what I could to help, the same as you."

Parthenia looked into the young man's kind eyes, and her stomach did a small flip. To her shame, she felt her face grow hot.

Scanlon said, "No, what you do is special. I'm just a grunt. Still, I thought maybe you wouldn't mind…"

Now it appeared to be his turn to grow embarrassed. His gaze turned downward and his cheeks reddened. He cleared his throat. "Would you like to have dinner with me? It would just be something from the printers, but I know how to…" He coughed again. "I mean, it's not much, but…"

She didn't answer immediately, too surprised to reply.

"It's okay," said Scanlon, stepping back. "This was a really dumb idea. It's just, I remember seeing your face, when I thought I was a goner, and you were so..." He sighed. "I can't explain it, but you looked...It meant a lot to me, and—"

"I'd like that," Parthenia interrupted. "Dinner," she added awkwardly.

"You're saying yes?" Relief and happiness broke over his features.

"Yes," she laughed. "I'm saying yes."

16

Carina had decided to get to know the *Bathsheba* intimately while she waited the eight months before she was to enter Deep Sleep. The vessel was vast, and if they were to come under attack, a detailed knowledge of her layout could be vital.

Carina had begun her tour at the highest point in the ship and then worked her way down to the Deep Sleep chamber where the main battle against Mezban's troops had been fought. It was one of two serving the same purpose, the other lying on the same level but the opposite side of the vessel.

She stood in the center of the room. The floor was as smooth and fresh as if it had been manufactured yesterday. All signs of the firefight had gone.

No one seemed to understand how the *Bathsheba's* interior surfaces self-repaired. She'd encountered plenty of self-*cleaning* starships—usually facilitated by nanobots—and most ships self-repaired to an extent, but she'd never known one that fixed itself on a microscopic level.

Her gaze roved the rows of egg-like structures that half-protruded from the walls: the stasis capsules. Many were now occupied by naked figures in fetal positions only just visible through the tinted shells.

Purely for convenience's sake, Mezban's troops and the rest of the prisoners had been ensconced in the lower levels. The upper lines of capsules were empty.

The sight brought back a childhood memory. Carina recalled one of the many insects she'd watched and studied when she was young, before Nai Nai died—a flying creature that lived in groups of hundreds and produced a deliciously sweet, sticky liquid. Her grandmother had said they were called bees.

Folk lore warned that the golden, viscous liquid was poisonous, but she'd suspected it was a white lie intended to discourage children from trying to take it. The small creatures would sting if they felt threatened. They built tiny chambers in layers to hold their precious fluid. Early in the year many of the cavities stood empty, but they would fill them all by the time the cool season arrived.

She'd Enthralled the bees to calm them, and then taken and eaten their liquid without coming to any harm.

The vacant and occupied Deep Sleep capsules reminded her of the bees' storage cells, only the contents of the filled capsules aboard the *Bathsheba* were not nearly so appetizing, though she hoped that Lomang and Mezban would prove as harmless as the bees had been.

They had both sent her savage looks when it came their turn to go into stasis. Lomang's polite subservience had disappeared, and Mezban had made threats of what she would do to Carina once she was free. Pappu had put up no resistance at all. Lomang's influence over his brother had always been clear, but in Mezban's presence he became positively submissive.

Calvaley had put up the biggest physical resistance, shouting and fighting with surprising vigor for a man his age. Perhaps it had been his excessive years that made him so reluctant to expose himself to the process. He hadn't said so, but perhaps he'd thought he was at a greater risk of never waking up. Perhaps he was right.

Now, he, like the others, floated in nutrient, his mind stilled and his bodily functions all but stopped.

What would it be like to experience Deep Sleep?

Carina sighed and strode out of the chamber. Her next stop was a second airlock on this level and the *Bathsheba's* largest portal. It was where Mezban's soldiers had boarded. Cadwallader had decided to leave the *Peregrine* attached to it for the duration of the voyage, reasoning that its position would hinder another enemy accessing the main airlock. Carina didn't think the *Peregrine* would present much of an obstacle to a determined attacker, and she would have preferred to secure the ship somewhere less easily accessible in the unlikely event Mezban escaped confinement, but Cadwallader had had the final say.

Carina was interested in the main airlock for another reason: it might have served as the entrance for the original passengers—the colonists on their way to a new planet. She wondered who they'd been, where they'd come from, and where they'd been heading.

How old was the ship? It was impossible to tell. The vessel retained no outer signs of wear and tear and the language its systems used was unrecognizable, so it was impossible to read the ship's log.

The Black Dogs' techs had suffered through days of difficulty trying to interact with the vessel's main computer. In the end, Carina had resorted to Enthralling Lomang and forcing him to help. He clearly did understand the strange language or he would not have been able to captain the ship. She made him translate some long texts in the *Bathsheba's* database into Universal Speech, thus teaching the computer how to understand the techs, rather than vice versa.

Later on, prior to putting the man into stasis, she'd asked him where he'd acquired the *Bathsheba*, but he'd refused to answer. At the time, it had seemed too much bother to Enthrall the man again, but now Carina wished she had. The procurement of such ships was a mystery.

Her ear comm suddenly sparked into life, making her jump.

"Lin, where are you?"

Cadwallader's customary gruff tone quickly dragged her out of her musings.

She answered his question, adding, "So the techs got the personal comm system working."

"Yes, finally. What are you doing down there?"

"Just looking around. I've been—"

"Come up to the Starlight Suite. We're having a celebration." He closed the comm.

The Starlight Suite was the name someone had given the *Bathsheba's* viewing dome, and the name had stuck.

Carina hadn't been there since she'd told Bryce she wanted to split up, and the thought of returning to the place, especially for a celebration, gave her a sickening feeling in the pit of her stomach.

She decided not to go. If Cadwallader had sanctioned a party, there would probably be alcohol and perhaps other substances involved, and after a while she wouldn't be missed. If he queried her tomorrow, she could say she'd attended but had only stayed a short while.

Her ear comm sprang to life again.

"That's an order," the lieutenant colonel said.

"Hey! You're not my CO. No one's my CO. I'm not a soldier anymore."

"Come on, Carina. Who are you trying to kid? You know you'll always be a merc at heart."

She blinked. Had she detected a slight slurring in the lieutenant colonel's speech?

"Sir, are you...drunk?"

"You see, you can't help calling me sir, can you? Come up here. You're missing all the fun."

In the years she'd known Cadwallader, she'd only seen him let his guard down a handful of times, and even then he'd only been somewhat less formal than usual.

Intrigue overcame her reluctance to attend a social gathering, and she headed for the nearest elevator.

THE STARLIGHT SUITE was filled with people. The artificial lights had been turned down to a mere glow, presumably to avoid losing the impact of the starscape above, and the dimly lit figures were occupying the lounge chairs and sofas, standing around in groups, or milling about. From the numbers present, Carina guessed most of the Black Dogs had to be there. Party music mixed with their chatter.

A tall figure was walking toward her. It took her a moment to recognize Cadwallader, and not only due to the low light. He was wearing a dark-colored sweater and slacks. It was the first time she'd ever seen him out of uniform.

"Glad you could make it, Lin."

"I couldn't disobey a direct order, could I?" She smiled wryly.

"Exactly. What do you want to drink?"

"I don't know. Something light. I probably won't stay long."

"Let's see what they have."

He led her through the throng of bantering mercs to the edge of the room, where a small crowd had gathered around a bar.

Cadwallader gave a loud cough, and the crowd parted to let him through.

He winked at Carina, saying, "Commander's privilege."

She was surprised by the array of drinks displayed at the back of the bar. The basic printed labels indicated they'd been created on the ship.

"What'll you have?" asked the bartender, who turned out to be Jackson.

"I don't know," she replied. "I don't know what half of those drinks are. I don't want anything too strong."

"I know just the thing."

Jackson took down a bottle and poured a measure of the liquid into a jug.

The lieutenant colonel leaned on the bar. "I figured you hadn't heard about the party when I noticed you weren't here. Even without the person-to-person comm working the news traveled fast."

"I don't think I've spoken to anyone today. I've been busy getting to know the ship."

"Smart idea," Cadwallader said.

Jackson had added two more drinks and ice to the jug. He screwed on the lid and shook it with his prosthetic arm so fast the jug became a blur.

"I knew a robot arm would come in handy one day," he quipped as he unscrewed the lid and poured the mixture into a glass. After pushing the glass toward Carina, he turned to serve someone else.

She sipped the cold cocktail. It was refreshing and light and not overly alcoholic.

"I have a couple of seats, over there." The lieutenant colonel indicated the far side of the room with a nod. "Care to join me?"

The reason he'd asked her to come to the celebration became apparent. He wanted to talk tactics. That was fine with Carina, though she felt a little duped. She could have completed her study of the ship and they could have talked tomorrow.

Cadwallader's seats were next to the wall at a point where

the transparent dome extended all the way down to the floor. The seats faced each other across a small, low table. To Carina's right, the black stretched out, seemingly to infinity. As she sat down, dizziness momentarily overcame her, and she clutched the chair arm, her drink slopping dangerously.

The lieutenant colonel reached over and took her other arm to steady her.

"It's quite the spectacle, isn't it?" he asked as she regained her balance and he released her.

"It sure is." She took another sip of her drink and then set it down on the table. Cadwallader refilled his glass from a half-empty pitcher.

He looked out into the emptiness of space. "When I'm aboard a starship, I sometimes forget *this* is what I'm traveling through."

The stars looked utterly motionless, though Carina guessed the *Bathsheba* had already built up considerable speed. The distances involved were too great for their movement to show.

"I know what you mean," she said.

The lieutenant colonel continued to stare into the starscape, appearing lost in thought.

"What's the celebration about?" she asked. "Is it because we took the ship?"

"Huh?" Cadwallader, returning to the present. "No. Tomorrow's the day most of the mercs go into stasis. I thought it wouldn't hurt to allow them to let their hair down a little. Ease their jitters."

"Oh, I get it. Makes sense. I confess I'm nervous about it myself."

He shrugged. "It's natural. From what I understand, the odds are a tiny minority won't wake up. Still, there are worse ways to die." His gaze returned to the void.

He seemed uncharacteristically pensive. Carina wondered when they were going to talk tactics.

Suddenly, he asked, "You knew Captain Speidel quite well, didn't you?"

She was taken aback. It hadn't occurred to her he might want to go over old times. Cadwallader was probably the least sentimental person she knew.

"I wouldn't say that," she replied. "More the other way around. He rarely talked about himself, but he was a great mentor. He saved my life. If I'd stayed where I was when he found me, I would probably be dead by now." *Or enslaved*, she added mentally. Stephan Sherrerr had told her once he'd been able to tell that Ma had borne a child, before he raped her and Parthenia was conceived.

It would have been just like him to seek out her mother's first born one day, eager to add her to his brood of mages.

"I'll always remember the dirty, scrawny ragamuffin John brought back to the ship. You looked like you hadn't seen soap or a hairbrush in several years, and you smelt as bad as you looked. It took all his powers of persuasion to convince Tarsalan to take you on. He threatened to resign if she refused."

Carina's throat tightened. "Really? I didn't know that."

"Well, you proved him right. You turned out to be a good soldier. A credit to our band."

"Thanks," she said quietly. "I owe it to Captain Speidel, though. I wouldn't be who I am without him." A lump was rising in her throat. "He would talk to me when no one else was around, sometimes. One-to-one, giving me advice and encouragement. He was like a father to me."

She'd been speaking softly, directing her attention to the black, unsure even if the lieutenant colonel could hear her. When she looked at him, however, she was shocked to see his eyes wet and glimmering.

"He was a good person," he said simply.

If Carina had ever doubted her suspicion that Speidel and

Cadwallader had been a lot more to each other than fellow offi-cers, those doubts were now cast aside.

"You must miss him," she said.

He pursed his lips and looked down.

She waited, leaving him to his emotions. She missed John Speidel too.

The party was growing rowdier, which was only to be expected among the Black Dogs. With luck, Atoi was some-where around and not too drunk to put a stop to things before they got out of hand. It would be a shame if Cadwallader was compelled to put his grief aside to deal with the unruly men and women.

The lieutenant colonel cleared his throat. "I haven't seen you with that young man recently. Have you two fallen out?"

"Bryce? No, we haven't fallen out exactly," she replied uneasily, confused by the sudden movement of the conversa-tion toward her love life. Was *this* why he'd asked her to go to the party?

He gazed at her steadily, waiting for more.

"I thought it was better to call things off between us."

"Why was that?"

Appearing to notice her discomfort, he added, "If you don't mind my asking."

Yes, I do mind.

"I just thought we would be better off apart," she said, and then closed her lips firmly, unprepared to say any more. She didn't dislike Cadwallader, but he wasn't Captain Speidel. She wasn't about to unburden herself to him about her self-doubt and dread of hurting the people she loved.

He tilted his head, his eyes searching her face.

When she maintained her silence, he said, "The black is a lonely place, Carina. If you find someone who's right for you and who believes in you, you should hold onto them. The opportunity may never come along again."

"Thanks for the advice," she said tightly. "I'll bear it in mind."

The corner of his lip lifted in a sad smile.

It was time for a change of subject. "I was wondering what we might come up against during the voyage?" she asked. "I don't know a lot about the Geriel Sector."

"I probably don't know much more than you. Perhaps we made a mistake in putting Lomang and Mezban into stasis so early. They might have been able to tell us what we can expect."

"Honestly, I'm reluctant to continue Enthralling Lomang. If you do it too much it can permanently damage the person's mind. But I guess I could have tried it with Mezban." She winced at the thought of using the Cast on the woman. Her fury afterward would be stupendous.

"It's too late now anyway," said Cadwallader. "Whatever happens, we'll have to face it the best we can. I also haven't discounted the possibility of the Sherrerrs tracking us down."

"You think they would come all this way just to avenge Sable Dirksen's death?"

"Maybe. It depends how much she meant to them."

"Should I ask Darius to Cloak the ship?" She hadn't asked her brother to perform his special Cast for a long time, imagining they must have left the evil clan behind weeks ago.

"Would he be able to Cloak a ship this size?" the lieutenant colonel asked in turn.

"I'm not sure." And it would be impossible to tell if Darius had managed to do it, as well as draining for the little boy to regularly make such powerful Casts.

"I think the odds of a Sherrerr attack are remote," said Cadwallader. "We'll have to take our chances."

"I guess so."

Carina hoped that if an attack were to come, it would happen in the next eight months, before she went into Deep Sleep.

17

After the crowded, noisy conditions on the *Duchess*, life aboard the *Bathsheba* had been an escape into silence and solitude even before the majority of the Black Dogs went into stasis. Once that part of the plan had been enacted, it became possible to pass entire days without encountering or hearing a single soul, which was exactly how Carina liked it.

Not that she didn't miss her siblings or Bryce, but her experiences had taught her that, in one way or another, she was a danger to them. The damage she'd done to their lives was irrevocable: Bryce had left his family and was journeying into a risky and unknown future and her siblings believed they were some kind of mage-soldiers who had an obligation to fight in every battle they encountered. Little Darius had nearly died, too, and it was all because of her.

If she couldn't persuade them away from the paths she'd set them on, the least she could do now was to keep her distance from them and avoid causing more damage.

As the days wore on and the *Bathsheba* crossed the galactic wilderness where star systems were few and habitable planets fewer, her days developed a set routine. She would wake early during the active shift and check in with Cadwallader for the latest updates—invariably there was little to report. Next she would work out, shower, and eat. Then she would tour the ship, checking the airlocks and the Deep Sleep chamber that held Mezban and her troops. Though the Black Dogs' techs had done a great job of familiarizing themselves with a deeply unfamiliar system, Carina still believed it might be possible for a Geriel Sector native to override the ship's computer without triggering an alarm.

After eating lunch alone at one of the many secluded food printing stations, she would spend her afternoons sifting through information in the vessel's database. She used the imperfect translation system the ship had developed with Lomang's help and, as time progressed and she grew more bored, she began to teach herself the new language. Her understanding increased accordingly.

One day, as she was digging deeper and deeper into the oldest archives, she came across a document entitled *Origins*. Scanning the text, she saw many words the computer couldn't translate but her new knowledge enabled her to guess the meanings of some of them.

Carina's eyebrows rose as she read. Assuming that the measurement of time in the Geriel Sector roughly corresponded with Standard Time, the vessel dated back fourteen hundred and seventy-one years. It hardly seemed possible. Perhaps the people who built the ship measured time differently from the system she knew.

The next part of the text related to why the *Bathsheba* had been built.

The first appearance of (untranslated) *is not recorded, but every century their numbers increased. They took the young worlds first, where life had barely begun. Our ancestors observed their practice but did nothing, imagining* (untranslated)*. Then they came to our* *planets, bringing* (a word Carina guessed might mean 'illness' or perhaps 'disease'). *We tried to reason with them, telling them their presence was a danger to us, but they did not listen. They told us their world was old and dying and they had nowhere else to go. This was not true. They had not even filled the first planets they settled on. It was only their greed that drove them on.*

More (untranslated) *continued to arrive. We tried to repel them, but our efforts were unsuccessful. Their weapons pierced us and burned us. Before that time we did not practice warfare. We had no technology or* (Carina figured the word here meant 'strategy') *to protect ourselves or fight back. As the years passed and we lost more and more battles and more land to the invaders, we learned new methods and invented weapons of our own. We also developed the* (untranslated).

We began to win. We began to kill the (untranslated). *We took back some of our land, but for generations the wars have continued. Warfare is now all our children know and all they can expect.*

But some of us do not wish to fight.

We cling to the ways of our forebears.

We seek a new (something like 'road').

We, the (untranslated), *built this space vessel* (untranslated – clearly it was Lomang or maybe an earlier owner who had named it *Bathsheba*) *to escape the invaders and the endless conflict. We will find a new world, a young planet, far from conflict and unnecessary death. We will settle there, practice the ways of the past, and live in peace.*

Carina sat back from the screen, amazed and intrigued by what she'd read.

Live in peace.

The people who had built the colony starship sounded like mages. And the vessel's surfaces self-repaired, unlike any other ship she'd known. Was that ability due to a long-forgotten Cast?

Was it possible that the first mages who had left Earth had

settled in the Geriel Sector? Had they remained there for thousands of years, living peaceful lives, until usurpers arrived and drove them from their homes? Maybe she'd been wrong about Ostillon being one of the first—if not *the* first—planet her ancestors had settled.

If mages had manufactured weapons and fought back against the invaders, that was an aspect of her culture that was new to her. The more she thought about it, it didn't sound like something they would do, and, except for the self-repairing feature, she hadn't encountered anything else about the *Bathsheba* that reminded her of her clan.

What seemed more likely was that the *Bathsheba's* builders and original passengers were from a different nonviolent group of people. Perhaps they had also left Earth during the early days of galactic colonization, and then later their settled worlds had been invaded by a later wave of more aggressive humans.

A horrible thought struck: had the newcomers deliberately passed on the infection? It would be an effective way to commit genocide, destroying the members of another civilization in order to take over their living space.

At least it appeared that all the events described in the database document had happened long ago. She didn't relish the idea of journeying through a war zone.

Nevertheless, the information could be important.

She comm'd Cadwallader. "Are you busy?"

"I have only twenty-five bored soldiers to command aboard a ship in the middle of nowhere," he replied. "What do you imagine I would be busy doing?"

"A simple 'no' would also work," Carina replied. "I found something interesting. I'm sending it to you, and I'm coming up for a chat."

∼

SHE HADN'T SEEN the lieutenant colonel in several weeks. His uniform was as crisp and neat as always, though the mercs she encountered occasionally around the ship were beginning to look sloppy and unkempt. She guessed it was hard to maintain high standards when the soldiers had very little to do. No dangers threatened them as far as they knew, and the ship looked after itself.

Morale was probably slipping, too—inevitable when you had a group of young, active men and women and nothing much for them to expend their energy on. It was just as well they would all be entering stasis in a few weeks.

Cadwallader looked up from his interface screen.

"I'm supposed to understand this?"

She'd forgotten she'd figured out the meaning of many of the words the computer hadn't translated into Universal Speech.

She gave him a rundown on what the text meant.

"That is interesting," he said, looking thoughtfully at the screen. "But this all happened ages ago, right?"

"I *think* so, but I still don't have a clear understanding of their chronometry."

"So it might still be relevant to us?"

"I guess it's possible these wars are going on even now." Carina paused as another potential concern popped into her mind. "There's something else—the *Bathsheba's* a massive ship. Not the kind of vessel that would be forgotten easily, even if she was built a long time ago. What if the original people who built her want her back? What if she's spotted and recognized?"

"In all the vastness of an entire galactic sector? That's *very* unlikely. On the other hand..." He strummed his lips. "...I don't like the sound of the aggressive race. They could have spread across the entire sector by now. I suppose it wouldn't hurt to increase the numbers out of stasis at any time. The troops won't thank me. It's going to mean more years awake for everyone. But it's better than being slaughtered while in Deep Sleep."

"I wonder if Lomang, Mezban, and the rest are descended from the invaders?" Carina wondered aloud.

Cadwallader shrugged. "There's no point in speculating. Thanks for bringing this to my attention, Lin. I'll think on it."

She left.

It was getting near dinner time. Usually in the evenings, after eating she would retire to her cabin in an otherwise-unoccupied residential section in a remote corner of the ship. There, she would spend the evening meditating and mentally rehearsing the Strokes, the Characters, the Seasons, the Map, and everything else Nai Nai had taught her.

Certain things, like the Map, had no real significance any longer, yet she found comfort and peace of mind in repeating the habits of her childhood.

Somewhat lost in reverie as she thought about the ancient war and the *Bathsheba's* builders, Carina almost didn't notice a movement ahead of her, where the corridor opened out to make room for an elevator tube.

When she looked more closely at the spot where she thought something had suddenly disappeared, it was empty.

She halted, her heart beginning to race. Sweat prickled on her skin.

What had she seen? Had enemies managed to board the ship?

Her hand moved to her side instinctively, but she wasn't carrying a weapon. As non-military personnel she wasn't required to and she'd gotten out of the habit.

Her elixir flask remained by her side, however. Removing it from its holder, she comm'd Cadwallader.

"What?" came his usual terse reply.

"I think we may have—oh, *shit!*"

Darius had stepped out from around the bend in the corridor.

"False alarm," Carina went on to the lieutenant colonel.

She sank to her knees as the little boy walked slowly closer, dragging his feet and looking down.

"Sweetheart, what is it? What's wrong?"

When he reached her, Darius lifted his head to meet her gaze.

"I Cast to find you, but I wasn't sure if it was okay to come and see you. The others don't know. You won't tell them, right?"

His big brown eyes were shiny.

"Of course I won't!" She pulled her brother into a hug and sat down on the floor with him on her lap, happiness and anguish coursing through her.

He rested his head on her chest. "I missed you."

"I've missed you too. So much. I've missed all of you."

"If you miss me, why don't you come and see me? Is it because Parthenia doesn't want you to?"

She heaved a deep sigh. "It isn't Parthenia's fault. It's just better this way. You know how you feel what I feel? I always seem to be angry or upset when I'm around you guys. I don't want to hurt you any more."

"It hurts more when you're not around," he said quietly.

An aching sob rose in her chest. She didn't want to cause him any more pain, the stars knew. She loved him deeply, the same as she loved all her brothers and sisters.

She was trapped. No matter what she did, she was the bane of her siblings' lives.

18

Darius's unhappiness sparked a change of heart in Carina. The following morning, she sat brooding in her cabin, wondering if she'd given up on her relationship with her family too soon. Now they were on their journey to Earth, perhaps she could avoid exposing them to danger, hurting them, and generally ruining everything. She decided to give things one last try.

But any potential reconciliation faced a major obstacle: Parthenia.

Her oldest sister was the one who had persuaded the others to shut her out, she was sure of it. And not without justification. She had crossed the line with Parthenia on more than one occasion, and though it had always been for the girl's safety and protection, she clearly didn't see it that way.

The girl had changed a lot since Carina had first gotten to know her. She had never been the meek, obliging character she'd portrayed to the world—that had been made evident the moment she'd helped to defeat the Sherrerr guards in the *Nightfall*, after the mage siblings had destroyed the Dirksen shipyard—but as time had passed she'd grown even stronger and more assertive.

And if Carina had harbored any doubt about the girl's inner steel, it had been put to bed when she'd punched their brother, Castiel, and escaped from Langley Dirksen's clutches without any help from anyone.

She had a huge amount of respect for Parthenia, yet somehow she seemed to have given her the opposite impression. If she could convince her of that and try to explain things from her own perspective, maybe they could find a way forward.

Before she'd moved her things to a cabin far distant from the suite her siblings occupied, in order to avoid the mutual embarrassment of bumping into them by accident, Carina had 'borrowed' something personal from each of them. These were not valuable items or anything that would be missed—a pencil that Darius had used, one of Oriana's hair pins, and so on. As well as serving as a small connection to the people she loved, Carina had also taken the things as a way of finding them in an emergency. Darius seemed to have done the same for her and maybe the other children, too.

Her need at the moment didn't exactly constitute an emergency, but it was important enough to warrant the mild invasion of privacy.

She reached under her bed and pulled out a box, lifting it onto her lap. She opened the lid. Among the rest of her family's personal artifacts inside lay several strands of hair she taken from Parthenia's comb. She took them out and wrapped them around her hand.

After closing her eyes, she Cast Locate.

The *Bathsheba*, gray and eerie, swam into focus in her mind's eye. The vast ship, its serried levels, and its pulsing engines were faintly illuminated lines in the dark void. Slightly brighter than the vessel's infrastructure were the individuals aboard her. Tiny figures moved along the corridors, rose up or sank down in the elevators, or congregated in the dining rooms, the viewing dome, and the gym. Others lay in their beds, sleeping before rising for the quiet shift, or floated in minute oval bubbles in the Deep Sleep chamber.

A single bright spark shone out: Parthenia was leaving the gym, and she seemed to be alone.

Perfect.

Carina would be able to speak to her in private, out of the hearing of their siblings. They could thrash out their problems and come to a better understanding.

She set off to see her sister.

PARTHENIA WAS PHYSICALLY DRAINED but happy after her session training in unarmed combat. Learning the moves wasn't difficult but she grew tired quickly when practicing them. The instructor, Atoi, had advised her to work out every day, focusing on building her upper body strength. She intended to follow the advice. She'd grown tired of trying to understand the sims —the characters spoke a foreign language that the computer translated really badly—and she'd gotten tired of spending most of her time with her brothers and sisters. They were kids and only interested in kids' stuff. A daily work out would give her something to do.

Not that she'd been spending *all* her time with her siblings, she reminded herself, a flush stealing over her face. After that first dinner with Kamil, when they'd talked for hours about where they'd come from, their lives before they'd ended up aboard the *Bathsheba*, and so many other things, most of which she'd forgotten, they'd met several more times.

Kamil was eighteen, she'd discovered, and he came from a planet deep within Dirksen territory. His country was cool and wet, he'd told her, and in the winter snow and ice lay on the ground four meters deep. The people wore long flat blades on their feet to help them get around, and, in the summer, everyone had to wear all-body suits to protect them from biting insects.

He'd wanted to try to find a place where the politicians weren't all corrupt and controlled by the Dirksen clan, but he hadn't had enough money to even get offplanet, so he'd joined the military.

Then he'd discovered the military was also in the pockets of the Dirksens, so as soon as he had the chance, when his unit had set down on another planet, Martha's Rest, he'd absconded. That had been when he'd joined the Black Dogs, while the band was preparing for the raid on Ostillon.

After hearing his story, Parthenia thought Kamil fit an awful lot into his eighteen years, but then, since her father had made the move to involve his family in the Sherrerr war with its rival clan, her life had been busy too.

At their fourth meeting, they'd kissed.

She felt her face grow even hotter with the memory.

"Parthenia!" a voice called from behind her.

She halted and, flustered, surreptitiously fanned her neck in an attempt to return her skin to its usual color.

"Hey, Parthenia," the person behind her said. "I was hoping I would find you here."

Knowing she was still embarrassingly red-faced, she turned around.

"How did the combat session go?" Kamil asked.

"Great," she replied. "Hard work, but really great."

"You look like you need a refreshing drink. Want to get one together?"

"I'd love to!"

They walked on.

"Who was coaching you?" asked Kamil.

When Parthenia told him, he grimaced and said, "She trained me too. She's a hard ass but I learned a lot."

"I didn't think she pushed us *too* hard. I mean, if it doesn't hurt, you're not improving, right?"

Kamil laughed. "You got that from her, didn't you?"

Parthenia replied, slightly defensively, "What if I did?"

Raising his hands, Kamil said, "I don't mean anything. It's just I remember her saying that." He spread his legs, stood on his tiptoes, put one hand on his hip, moved his shoulders back, waggled a finger at Parthenia and said in a deep voice, "If it don't hurt, you're not improving."

She chuckled.

"So, what did you learn?" asked Kamil as they continued walking.

"We focused mostly on defense today."

"WANT TO SHOW ME SOME MOVES?"

"Sure," said Parthenia, happy to show off what she'd learned. "Why don't you try to grab me from behind?"

"Okay, walk a little way ahead."

She walked a few paces farther, listening for Kamil's approach. She'd expected him to run at her, but she couldn't hear him so she guessed he was going to try to surprise her.

Suddenly, his arm dropped over her face.

He was going for a choke hold.

Before he had a chance to get a good grip, she pushed her chin toward her chest, forcing his arm away from her neck. He wasn't pressing in forcefully. She went to elbow him in his stomach—not too hard—but before she had time to make contact, she heard the crack of a blow on flesh.

Kamil's hold on her was instantly released.

A body hit the floor.

Parthenia spun around.

Kamil was sprawled out and Carina was standing over him, drawing her elbow back, preparing to punch him again.

Parthenia screamed and leapt at her sister. "What the hell are you doing? Leave him alone!" She grabbed Carina's arm.

"He was trying to hurt you!" Carina shouted, struggling with her. "I'm gonna make him regret it!"

Kamil was stirring. He sat up and shook his head. Then he noticed the sisters fighting. A look of alarm on his face, he scooted away from them on his butt.

"He's my friend!" Parthenia exclaimed as she wrestled with her sister. "I was showing him what I learned at combat training today, you idiot!"

"Huh?" Carina said, then she seemed to finally understand as she stopped trying to break free.

"I think you misunderstood," said Kamil, standing up and rubbing a spot above his ear.

"He's my friend," Parthenia repeated, tears of anger and shame spilling from her eyes. She pushed Carina away from her. "Why do you always have to interfere? *Why*? Why can't you leave me alone?"

"I-I saw him attack you," Carina faltered. "I just thought...I wanted to protect you."

"When are you going to understand I don't need your help? I don't *need* you!"

"Parthenia," Kamil said gently, "I'm sure it was an honest mistake. Anyone seeing what I did wouldn't have known—"

"It wasn't you, it was her!" she exclaimed. "She's always butting in, trying to control everything I do, always overreacting. I'm sick of it!"

"Okaaay, I think I'd better give you two some space," Kamil said. "No hard feelings," he added to Carina before leaving.

Parthenia faced her sister, her hands clenched at her sides.

Carina said, "I'm s—"

"For the last time, leave me alone," Parthenia said between

her teeth. "I don't want to have anything to do with you ever again. Stay out of my life!"

Her sister went to speak, but she changed her mind. She nodded, and then walked away.

Parthenia drew in a shuddering breath and wiped her eyes.

Maybe this time Carina would finally get the message.

19

The time had finally come. Carina faced the open, empty Deep Sleep capsule. She was alone on an upper tier in the chamber except for one of the Black Dog's medics, who sat at the entrance, interface in hand, checking the list of who was to enter stasis that day.

Never in her life had she undergone anything resembling Deep Sleep. She hadn't even had an operation or any other medical procedure—Nai Nai had warned her to avoid splicers at all costs, fearful that they might investigate her genome and discover something odd and unique to mages. From that moment onward, she would be on the slippery slope to captivity and enslavement, or torture, if she refused to 'perform'.

The fact that one of Mezban's soldiers had already died didn't help her feelings of trepidation. The man had been entirely normal and healthy, yet the capsule had signaled he was passing away. Though the medics got him out and treated him in record time, nothing had worked. He'd never woken up; never knew he was dying. Perhaps that was for the best.

She looked around the chamber. The capsules in the lower

tiers were already filled with mercs, many of whom had entered stasis soon after the voyage began. Cadwallader had entered his, too, leaving Atoi in charge, and so had Carina's brothers and sisters.

She remembered the farewells of her siblings with painful clarity.

The previous months of rarely even seeing her brothers and sisters, let alone interacting with them, had been difficult to endure. She'd thought her years of living alone on the street as a child had accustomed her to a solitary life, and that was probably true, but when it came to her siblings, she'd found being apart from them torturous.

She'd missed them all deeply, and every night she'd worried about their welfare, rarely getting more than a few hours' sleep. Yet after the embarrassing incident with Parthenia, she'd ceased questioning the wisdom of her self-imposed separation.

There was no doubt in her mind that she was bad news for her brothers and sisters.

Yet when she'd encountered them all again outside the Deep Sleep chamber, the difficulties of the past eight months had faded to nothing. Faced with the prospect of never seeing each other again, they had clung to each other as tightly as if the hull had breached and depressurization was trying to rip them apart.

Except for Parthenia. She'd stood away from her siblings as they'd each hugged goodbye, glowering.

Now, they were all nestled in stasis chambers like baby birds in translucent eggs. She hoped to the stars she would see them all again. Perhaps she could still find a better way forward with them, once they woke up.

Five years from now.

Their capsules had been programmed to wake them up five years hence. After that, she and her family would live out several months aboard the ship before entering Deep Sleep again.

At the meeting where the rota had been decided, Cadwallader had suggested dividing the mages into two groups to spread out the benefit of their powers to the ship's defense, but Carina and Parthenia had argued as one that the family should never be split up.

She gazed at the smooth, pale gray interior of the place where she would spend the next five years. Tiny holes peppered the inner surface, from which the liquid nutrient would spray after the capsule sealed. Before that happened, she should already be unconscious.

From what she'd heard, the experience was supposed to be like falling asleep and waking up again, though complete recovery took about a week.

She thumped the heel of her hand against her forehead.

That was enough speculation. It was time to get in.

"Carina!"

Bryce.

His voice had come from below. She turned and peered over the railing. He was walking across the floor of the chamber.

"Wait there," he said. "I'm coming up."

A realization hit her like an explosive going off—*this* was why she had delayed entering stasis.

As his footsteps echoed on the metal treads, a surge of relief washed over her. She *couldn't* go into stasis without saying goodbye to him. They'd hardly spoken as the months had passed, just small talk or the necessary conversations related to ship's business. He'd seemed okay, but whenever they spoke it was like he'd been holding something back. But then maybe the same had been true of her.

He emerged onto the walkway. "Carina, I..."

She stepped quickly toward him and fell into his arms.

For several moments, she couldn't speak. Bryce also said nothing.

"I just had to see you before you—"

"I know, I know," said Carina. "I'm glad you came."

She luxuriated in his embrace, wishing she could stand there forever.

"When do you go in?" she asked.

"Tonight. A couple of hours from now." His hug tightened. "Stay safe, okay? I couldn't bear it if I never saw you again."

"Me either," Carina whispered.

"Then why the distance between us? I mean, I do understand why...what you're afraid of. But what you think isn't true. You're too hard on yourself."

"Yeah, maybe you're right. I think I can see that now." She felt like she was drowning, choking. She'd never doubted how much she loved him. It was *because* of that she'd kept away. But maybe she'd been wrong. Or was she being selfish, wanting to be with him knowing that he would end up hurt?

Holding him felt too good. She had to break away or she might never manage it.

"I have to go," she murmured.

"I know."

His arms slipped away from her as he looked her intently in the eyes. "When we wake up, we'll try again, right?"

Anxiety and doubt rushed up from her stomach, but she swallowed them down. "Yes. Let's try."

He grinned, leaned forward, and kissed her lips. "It'll be like waking up tomorrow. I'll see you tomorrow, okay?"

Then he turned and strode away. When he reached the floor, he waved before leaving the chamber.

Her apprehension eased, Carina faced the capsule once more. If she didn't survive stasis, at least she'd made her peace with the people she loved.

She took off her clothes, folded them, and placed them on

the shelf next to the opening. She put her flask of elixir on top of the pile, though she was unsure if the liquid would remain effective for years.

Step in, sit down, and wait. That's the trigger that activates the Deep Sleep process. The chamber does the rest. That's what the tech had said.

She climbed in. The base was smooth and cool under her bare feet.

A soft hum sounded. The outer half of the shell swung inward and closed with a snick. She was shut inside the small space.

She was not unconscious. *Why wasn't she unconscious yet?*

Panicking, she tried to stand up but hit her head on the ceiling.

Why wasn't stasis working?

Was it because she was a mage? Other apparatus hadn't worked on her in the past, like the weapon she'd stolen on Banner's Moon, when she'd been working for the Sherrerrs. It had incapacitated all the other soldiers with terror, but she'd felt no effects.

If the process wasn't working for her due to her difference from other humans, that would mean it hadn't worked for her mage siblings! She'd thought they were in Deep Sleep, but they could be dead, drowned in nutrient.

She braced herself against the inner wall and kicked the outer shell with both feet, but the seal remained firmly intact.

The tiny nozzles sprang to life, spraying her in a cool, viscous liquid.

Carina screamed, and then knew no more.

20

C arina woke, freezing, wet, and naked.

Hands were grabbing her, hauling her. She writhed, trying to break free, and slipped, landing hard on a cold, metal surface. Her sodden hair hung in ropes over her face, blocking her vision, her eyes weren't working properly anyway. Everything looked blurry and all that she could hear sounded muffled and distant. She could make out shouting and cries of pain and distress, but they were distorted as if she was listening through glass.

She tried to stand, tried to get a grip on the smooth floor, but the mucusy liquid coating her made her slip. Then a massive hand fastened on her shoulder and brute strength forced her downward until she squirmed on her stomach.

"Stay down," a deep, husky voice breathed hotly in her ear. "Stay still, if you know what's good for you."

She knew that hand, that voice. It was Pappu.

Lomang and Mezban had escaped stasis!

The giant had gained his freedom, and he was back to his old state, all submissiveness gone now that his brother and Mezban were in charge again.

She stopped struggling, knowing her efforts were pointless against Pappu's brawn. She squeezed her eyes shut and opened them again several times, trying to make them work. The nutrient fluid had seeped under her lids and covered her eyeballs, but her vision problems were more than that—she hadn't used her eyes since entering stasis, possibly as long as five years previously.

Her right cheek pressed against the floor, and her hair drooped over her face. She lifted a hand to move it away and was rewarded by renewed pressure on her back from Pappu. She grunted and dragged her hair from her eyes.

The opposite side of the Deep Sleep chamber was revealed to her, though the lights bloomed into fuzzy, pale yellow suns, and the lines of the walkways and capsules were undefined. Figures moved along the walkway, opening capsules and pulling out their occupants.

Sounds were becoming clearer.

Carina realized the voices she heard were speaking a foreign language—that was partly why she hadn't been able to make out what they were saying

Yet when she concentrated harder, she found she did understand them. They were speaking the language of the *Bathsheba.*

"Here he is!" someone shouted.

"You're sure?" a voice replied.

Lomang.

"Yes, I recognize him."

"Fine," Lomang said. "Do it before he comes around."

A horrible, sickening crunch resounded, followed by the dull thump of a limp body hitting the floor.

It sounded like someone had died.

Who was *he*?!

Who had Lomang ordered to be killed?

She fought to rise.

"Stay where you are!" Pappu barked in Universal Speech.

"Get off me, you bastard! Let me up. If any of you have hurt one of my brothers..."

"It was not your brother!" Pappu hissed. "I'm telling you, if you value your life and your family's lives, do not move!"

Carina collapsed, forcing down despair. If it wasn't Ferne or Darius, could it have been Bryce?

People were moving on the walkway opposite. Men and women in uniform—she finally recognized Mezban's troops—were forcing the groggy and disoriented mercs taken out of stasis to their feet and attempting to march them out of the chamber, though many could barely walk.

Pappu's large hand was an implacable force on her back, pressing her down so hard she was having trouble breathing.

"Darius!" she called out. "Ferne! Parthenia! Any of you! Are you okay?"

"Your siblings are not here! Be quiet, or I will make you quiet."

She knew too well how easily Pappu could make good on his promise, so she stopped resisting—for now. As soon as she got a hold of some elixir, she would put everything right again, only this time Lomang, Mezban, Pappu, and probably the rest of their troops too, would be spaced.

When the chamber seemed mostly empty and her vision and hearing had returned to normal, the pressure on her back lifted, and Pappu's paw fastened around her bicep. He hoisted her to her feet with the ease of picking up trash from the floor.

As soon as she was upright, however, she immediately collapsed. Her legs wouldn't bear her weight. They felt like jelly and as she looked down, she saw her thigh muscles were wasted.

Pappu lifted her again and began dragging her toward the

steps. She stumbled, trying to get her legs underneath her as her feet scraped along the floor.

She was now shivering in the cool chamber, all the residual heat from the stasis capsule fluid dissipating into the atmosphere as she'd been forced to wait for the others to leave.

Then she saw him.

She screamed.

The meager strength in her lower limbs evaporated and she hung, limp, in the giant's grasp, sobbing.

A few meters in front of her lay a man's body, utterly still. The back of his head had been destroyed and his sightless eyes gazed upward.

Cadwallader was dead.

Before he'd even had time to properly return to consciousness, Lomang's order had ripped the man's life from him.

"Stand up!" Pappu ordered. "Yes, your commander was executed. What did you expect? If it weren't for your powers you would be dead too. Now, move!"

Grief enveloped her.

The lieutenant colonel had been a hard man and difficult to get to know, but his position dictated that. He'd always been honorable, principled, and self-sacrificing, and she'd glimpsed another side of him—a softer side. If they'd had more time, she might have gotten to know him well, and that would have been to her benefit, not his. But now that time would never come.

The next few minutes passed in a blur as the giant yanked her the rest of the length of the walkway, past Cadwallader's body, down the stairs, and out of the chamber.

She felt like an animal on a leash, only the leash was her arm and the collar was her shoulder. Pappu's grip was a band of iron around her bicep, cutting off the blood to the rest of her limb.

Suddenly, rage flared up in her.

"Where is my family?! Where's Bryce?! If you've hurt them, I'll kill all of you!"

She tried to wrench herself free, but even if she hadn't been in her weakened state, her strength was no match for the giant's.

Instead, she bit his hand, grinding her teeth into his flesh.

Pappu roared.

He let go of her, and she dropped like a bag of stones.

His bloody hand drew back and then swept toward her. His knuckles cracked against her jawbone, snapping her head around.

The world receded, turning black. As she edged back from unconsciousness, she became vaguely aware of pain emanating from her face, but she leapt at the giant, power surging miraculously into her wasted legs.

But Pappu caught her deftly by the throat and lifted her up.

She dangled like a doll, choking, fingers scrabbling uselessly at the giant's thick digits.

"Ah, little lady," he said softly. "How I would love to squeeze the life out of you." He drew her closer. "I haven't forgotten how you left me in the grip of the mech. You poured shame on me, purposefully, and one day I will make you pay—slowly."

He lowered her until the tips of her toes brushed the floor.

"But today is not that day."

His hand left her throat, but before she could collapse, he lifted her by her waist and slotted her under his arm.

"Be warned, you belligerent woman. I may not be at liberty to kill you, but I can make you suffer."

As she hung awkwardly in Pappu's grasp, she tried to think of another way to hurt him, but then she remembered Bryce's words when Lomang's men had first surprised them on Ostillon. He'd pleaded with her, telling to stop fighting, that she was going to get herself killed.

He'd been right, and the same applied now.

Expending the little energy she had on resisting Pappu was pointless and dangerous.

She would wait, find out what was happening and what Lomang and Mezban intended. Then she would wait for the right moment and strike.

This time, there would be no mercy.

21

L omang and Mezban sat side by side in the *Bathsheba's* gym hall, their quarrels apparently forgotten or put aside. Somehow, Lomang had managed to find his ridiculous blue hat and had it perched on his head. Ten or twelve of Mezban's troops stood behind them.

Carina peered at the men and women at the rear of the hall, sensing something not quite right about them.

Pappu had set her down as he'd entered the room. He pushed her and she stumbled forward, ending up on her hands and knees, her muscles still weak.

She raised her head.

Mezban's look was imperious, but Lomang's was inscrutable. He nodded at a woman standing at the edge of the gym. She walked over to Carina, carrying a cloth over her outstretched arms.

The woman bent down, offering her the textile.

After a brief moment of confusion, she took it and wrapped it over her shoulders. The piece of material was sufficiently large to cover her to her knees. With some difficulty, she stood.

"Where are my brothers and sisters? Where is my friend, Bryce? What have you done with them?"

"Our positions have exchanged now," said Lomang. "It is myself and the magnificent Mezban Noran, Procurator of the Majestic Isles, Member of the Encircling Council, who will ask the questions, and you will answer."

"I'm not telling you anything until I know the people I love are safe."

She heard a heavy footfall from behind, then Pappu's hand clasped her head, his fingers reaching around to squeeze her cheeks, pressing painfully into the bruise forming where he'd hit her.

"I think I can crush her skull with one hand, brother," he said. "Would you like me to try?"

His grip tightened.

"You aren't going to kill me," said Carina. "So don't bother threatening. You need me."

Mezban leaned forward, narrowing her eyes. "We may not want you dead, but that won't stop us from hurting you."

"Oh, quit the dramatics!" Carina exclaimed.

She blinked.

The reason why Mezban's soldiers looked odd had hit her.

She twisted her neck, wrenching her head out of Pappu's hand.

"What's going on here?" she demanded.

She looked behind her and through the exits. Only the giant stood to her rear and the doorways were empty and dark.

She tightened the cloth over her shoulders and took a step forward.

"Remain still!" yelled Mezban.

Pappu laid his heavy hands on her again.

"Let me go!" She felt like screaming in frustration. "Tell me who's really in charge here! I'll speak to them, not you."

"Bring her closer," said Lomang.

Pappu pushed her over to Lomang and Mezban.

"Tell me who's giving you orders!" Carina demanded. "Is it the Sherrerrs? Did Kee catch up to us?"

"No one is giving us orders," said Mezban. "You are under our command now, and you will do as we say."

Lomang touched his wife's arm, as if to caution her or remind her of something.

"What makes you think we are under another's direction?" he asked.

"Your soldiers aren't armed! And someone killed Cadwallader with a blow to his head, not a pulse round. If you're the ones in control around here, where are your troops' weapons?"

"Why would I arm my troops if we have control of the ship?" Mezban countered.

"Because you have more than a hundred trained and experienced mercs you just took out of stasis. Only a moron wouldn't arm their guards. And I don't *think* you're that stupid."

Fury flared in Mezban's features and she spluttered with rage.

"Calm yourself, my love," Lomang said to her. "Her words are the twittering of a bird in a cage."

He continued in the foreign language, no doubt imagining Carina couldn't understand him, "And yet...she does have a point."

"What *point* is that?" asked Mezban viciously in the same language.

"Her correct assumption that we are not the true masters of this vessel will impact her willingness to work with us. Without her cooperation, the—" he said a word Carina didn't recognize "—may see fit to sell us as a delicacy, rather than as slaves."

"I don't like the bitch," Mezban muttered. "We should have killed her and kept the children. They're enough of a bargaining tool."

"My dear," Lomang urged, "the children are too scared.

Their fear robs them of their ability. This one may be our salvation."

As the conversation had gone on, Mezban had been steadily glaring at Carina. Suddenly, her look sharpened and a new understanding lit her face. "I think she comprehends us!"

Carina tried to maintain a blank expression, but she didn't appear to convince the woman of her ignorance.

Mezban drew away from Lomang and jabbed a finger at Carina. "Do you speak our language?" she asked in Universal Speech.

There was no point in dissembling. Now Mezban suspected Carina understood she would never be careless in speaking around her again.

"I understand a little," said Carina. "Enough to know I'm a *bitch*."

Mezban scowled.

Lomang rested his elbows on his knees as he leaned forward to speak to her.

Carina was shocked to see his paunch hang down between his spread thighs. The last time she'd seen the smuggler, he'd thinned all the way down to a normal weight.

How long had he been out of stasis? Certainly long enough to put on some fat.

How long have I been in Deep Sleep?

"Perhaps there is a little truth to your guess," he said to her. "What if I were to tell you that there are other masters—even more powerful than Mezban and myself—who would be interested in what you and your siblings can do? And that the knowledge of this power could mean the difference between life and death for all of us?"

"I would say I see no reason why my ability should save *you*," she replied fiercely.

"I *told* you not to talk to her!" Mezban blurted. "You fool! Idiot!" She struck her husband with the side of her fist.

"Please, my darling, have patience. There are many roads we may travel yet, and none can foresee all ends."

"I see an end for you!" yelled Mezban. "And if *they* don't do it, I will!"

She jumped out of her seat and strode away, her little legs and arms swinging.

Lomang sighed, but his gaze followed her adoringly.

The small woman neared a doorway, but then abruptly halted. All anger and indignation appeared to ooze out of her, and she took a step back, her arms dangling at her sides, her jaw hanging loose.

Lomang slowly rose to his feet. "Mezban, my love, come here." His tone was soft and fearful.

But his wife seemed frozen. She only stared at something beyond the door.

Though Carina couldn't see the object of her fear, the feeling was infectious. She shivered under the cloth she was clutching tightly to her chest.

The gazes of the soldiers at the end of the gym were fixed on the black opening.

A squeak escaped Mezban's lips, and she dropped to her knees.

A long, slim, dark gray limb clad in exoskeleton entered the room.

Horror clasped Carina's throat.

The limb was followed by another, and then a third.

A searing silence permeated the atmosphere. The only sound was the click of the creature's limbs on the tiled floor.

Carina had heard tales of these aliens when she was a child —terrible tales of abhorrent acts, of children murdered, of people being eaten alive, of entire towns depopulated.

The stories had been so awful, she'd begun to suspect the beings were made up, that nothing could be so evil.

But then, when she was nine years old, they had attacked

the small, impoverished settlement where she lived. She'd seen the dreadful things with her own eyes and witnessed the truth of their rumored ability to time-shift. She'd seen they were real.

Commander Kee had not caught up to the *Bathsheba*, set on revenging the death of Sable Dirksen, and nor had some traitor among the Black Dogs wakened Lomang and Mezban from their Deep Sleep. Their release was due to another event entirely: the arrival of an enemy of all humankind.

The ship had been taken over by Regians.

22

"Carina!"

Darius leapt up and ran toward her.

"I can't hug you," she said, looking down at the cloth she was gripping to her chest. "This is all I'm wearing."

"But I can hug you!" the little boy announced.

She bent down, and he wrapped his arms around her neck, tugging her lower.

Two of Mezban's unarmed guards and Pappu had brought her to a suite of rooms, pushed her through the door, and then closed and locked it.

To Carina's immense relief all her siblings were inside, and they showed no signs of any injuries. Ferne and Oriana were lying on the floor, an interface screen between them, and Parthenia was standing behind Nahla, a hairbrush in her hand.

When Carina caught her oldest sister's eye, she looked away quickly and continued to brush Nahla's hair.

"I'm *so* glad you're okay!" Oriana exclaimed. Ferne echoed the sentiment, and both the twins also came over to welcome her with a hug.

But when Nahla did the same, Parthenia remained where she was.

"I'll find you some clothes," she said stiffly and then walked into a bedroom.

"We were hoping Mezban would take you out of stasis," said Ferne. "We were worried about you."

"She was saying she was going to leave everyone else in the capsules until we reach our destination, wherever *that* is," Oriana said.

Suddenly, Carina's last few drops of energy were expended, and she tottered, unable to stand any longer.

"Whoa," said Ferne as she collapsed in his direction. He caught her and, with help from Oriana, supported her as far as the sofa.

She fell into the seat and lay against the cushions.

Parthenia returned from the bedroom carrying a pair of pants and a shirt.

"Wait a minute," Oriana said. "I know something better."

She ran into another room and came out again with a coverlet and a pillow.

"Remember how weak we were when we woke up?" she asked the others generally as she placed the covering over Carina. "Just rest for a bit. You'll feel better in a few days." She put the pillow at the end of the sofa. "Lie down if you want to."

"Thanks." Carina's happiness at seeing that her brothers and sisters were okay momentarily overcame her fears about their perilous situation. Then she recalled something she wanted to ask them. "When you all went into stasis, did it seem like you remained awake too long?"

"Yes!" Ferne replied. "It was really scary. I thought I was going to die! But then I must have gone unconscious. We talked about it when we were woken up, right?" he said to the others.

"Yeah, it was horrible," said Oriana.

"The same thing happened to me," Carina said. "I think it's

something to do with our genetics. I had a similar experience before, though at the time it was to my advantage. I'm glad you were all okay in the end."

"The stasis capsules automatically evacuate if the subject begins to suffer a medical emergency," said Parthenia. "I don't think we were in any danger."

"I'm sure you're right," Carina smiled at her sister, but Parthenia returned her gaze stonily. "You'll have to fill me in on everything that's happened. I only woke up about an hour ago. But, before we go into that, where's Bryce? Have any of you seen him?"

"No," Parthenia answered gravely. "We don't know where he is."

Concern over Bryce reminded Carina of another man, someone none of them would ever see again.

"I have some bad news," she said. Then, because there was no easier, gentler way of saying it, she added, choking as she spoke, "Lieutenant Colonel Cadwallader is dead."

"Oh no!" Oriana clasped her cheeks, her eyes filling with tears.

"Lomang gave the order for him to be executed," she continued. "I heard it as I was coming out of Deep Sleep." She decided not to mention she'd seen his dead body, especially not in front of Nahla.

"He was a nice man," Nahla said, sadly.

Carina nodded. She doubted any of his soldiers would have described Cadwallader as 'nice', but he'd always been kind to the children. And though he'd been a tough, strict commander, no one could have accused him of being unfair.

She recalled the party in the viewing dome, when he'd tried to give her advice about her relationship with Bryce. She bit her lip as she recalled how she'd rebuffed him. He'd only been trying to help, and he'd been right when he'd said something like that was worth holding onto. Maybe she'd been too hasty in pushing Bryce and her family away. Maybe this time she could help them without screwing up.

She beckoned Nahla closer. As she grasped the little girl's hand in her own, she said, "How have you been feeling, sweetie? Do you still have nightmares?"

"Sometimes." Nahla's gaze turned downward.

"Not so much anymore," Parthenia said. "I think she's getting better."

Carina wasn't sure her youngest sister would ever get over being trapped with Stevenson's body in the pilot's cabin. She felt bad she hadn't been around to help her during those eight months they'd waited to go into stasis.

Perhaps sensing her feelings, Darius said brightly, "Nahla's my best friend. Look at the pictures we drew together. Do you like them?"

He was pointing at a wall, and Carina noticed for the first time that several pieces of paper had been stuck to it, each a hand-drawn image. She saw stick figures, starships, castles, and eggs with people inside, which she assumed to be depictions of the time the children had spent in stasis.

"I love them! Did you draw them all by yourselves?"

Darius and Nahla nodded proudly.

Then Carina saw a picture that was not so pleasant. A black, many-legged creature loomed over a group of stick figures of different sizes.

So the kids had met the Regians. She shuddered at the thought. They must have been utterly terrified.

"Nahla's a chatterbox now," Ferne said.

The little girl pouted, so he added, "In a nice way."

"Yes, we love hearing Nahla talk," said Oriana. "She tells stories."

"*Amazing* stories," Darius said expansively.

"Well," said Carina, "there's a particular story I need to hear. What's been happening while I was in Deep Sleep? How long have you all been out of stasis and what's happened to you?"

From what Lomang and Mezban had implied, it appeared they'd attempted to impress the Regians with her siblings' mage powers, but the children had been too upset to Cast, understandably.

"I think that's a story *I* should tell you," Parthenia said solemnly, "and perhaps out of the hearing of little ears."

"Hmm," said Ferne, "I think that's a hint we need to take Darius and Nahla to play a game in our bedroom."

"I do believe you're right, brother," Oriana quipped.

The twins' cheerfulness despite the circumstances warmed Carina's heart, but Parthenia's expression soon cooled it again.

After a little protesting, Darius and Nahla followed their brother and sister into a bedroom.

Parthenia watched until the door closed, then she turned to Carina.

"We were brought out of Deep Sleep three and a half weeks ago. After giving us a day to recover, Lomang told us to make elixir, then he took us one by one to some horrible creatures..." her face twisted with disgust "...and instructed us to Cast. He took me first, and I pretended to be too afraid to do it. I told the others to do the same. I don't think Darius had to even fake it. Those aliens are terrifying. And, of course, Nahla can't Cast anyway. Lomang didn't believe me when I told him but he seems to think she's also too scared."

"You were *pretending* you couldn't Cast?" Carina was impressed. Her sister's tactic had been smart. The idea that the Regians were so horrifying the children couldn't Cast was entirely believable.

If she'd been in her sister's place, she would have defied Lomang and *refused* to Cast, no doubt bringing down a world of trouble on her head.

"That was a great idea," she continued.

"Thanks, but I don't need your praise," Parthenia replied acidly.

Carina inwardly winced.

"Anyway," said Parthenia, "since then he's tried the same thing again, several times, but our weeping and wailing must be pretty convincing because now he's woken *you* up. He probably thinks you're tougher than us."

"Maybe. He and Mezban wanted to question me about something, too, but our conversation didn't get that far in the end. Has Lomang said anything about what's going on, or have you overheard anything?"

"Nothing. He always speaks his own language when he isn't talking directly to us, and we spend most of our time in here anyway. The soldiers bring us food twice a day. I've been trying to keep everyone occupied so they don't worry too much."

"You..." Carina hesitated. She didn't want to upset her already prickly sister. "...I really don't mean this in a patronizing way, but you've done a great job. Ma would be proud."

Parthenia didn't reply, but neither did she look angry.

"I'll tell you what I know, okay?" Carina went on. "Then we can decide *together* what to do next."

"Okay," Parthenia replied, uncertainly.

"I've encountered Regians once before, when I was a little girl. They prey on humans, attacking small, remote settlements on insignificant planets and capturing as many of the inhabitants as they can find. No one they captured has ever escaped, so nobody knows exactly what happens to the people who are taken. As I understand it, it's been going on for centuries. The stories had passed into folklore where I grew up, and I never quite believed them. Until they came to my town."

Parthenia's mouth gaped in horror. "Couldn't the local army fight them off?"

"There *was* no army where I lived. I guess the Regians deliberately target places where they'll meet little resistance, but even if we'd had weapons and trained soldiers, they're difficult to defeat. They have a special capability: they can move forward and backward in time, just by a second or so. It makes them hard to kill. You could have the perfect shot, but by the time your round reached them, the creature wouldn't exist in that moment anymore. When it did return to the exact present, the round would have passed through the space it was occupying. Does that make sense?"

"I think so."

"The good news for us is their ability doesn't make them immune from a Cast. Do you know why?"

Parthenia's eyes grew thoughtful, then her features brightened. "Because Casts work slower than pulses?"

"You got it. The lag—the thing that's usually a disadvantage to us—is actually an advantage when it comes to killing Regians. Their time-shift isn't sufficient to avoid the slower effect of a Cast."

Her sister's nose wrinkled. "Do we have to kill them?"

Carina put a hand on her shoulder. "I know it isn't going to be easy, but it's them or us."

23

M ezban's troops came for Carina in the middle of the quiet shift the second day after she'd come out of stasis, when she was sound asleep. Though the guards were weaponless, their numbers and strength made resisting them foolish, and she didn't want to upset her siblings by putting up a fight.

Instead, she went quietly, rising from the sofa she was using as a bed and allowing one of the five soldiers to lead her away. She felt terrible, even worse than she had during the first hours after she'd come out of stasis. She'd regained some strength in her legs, but an exhaustion had settled on her that sleep didn't erase, her muscles ached no matter what position she lay in, and just the thought of eating made her gag.

Only Parthenia woke up as she was leaving. Her sister watched from her open bedroom door as Carina left, raising her hand in a silent farewell.

It was clear what lay in store: Lomang and Mezban were going to try to make her Cast in front of the Regians. From what she'd understood, it appeared that this was intended to impress the creatures and prevent them from slaughtering all the humans aboard the *Bathsheba*.

From Carina's perspective, the smuggler and his wife were indulging in wishful thinking. Even if she'd been inclined to protect them from the aliens—which she surely was not—the creatures were not dumb. Why would they place any value on the humans who couldn't Cast? It would make more sense to set aside the ones who could, and then kill the rest.

The thought of the wholesale murder of everyone aboard made her shudder. She might be able to trick the Regians into believing that Nahla could Cast and so should be allowed to live, but what about Bryce, Atoi, and the rest of the mercs? And the soldiers under Mezban had only been following orders—she had no personal gripe against them.

Another thought struck: where was Jace? She hadn't seen him for months prior to going into stasis. She'd been angry with him for siding with Cadwallader about forming a council. The children hadn't mentioned him either. Did Lomang and Mezban even know he was a mage? He'd helped in the defense of the *Duchess's* airlock during Mezban's attack, but the woman had been in the viewing dome at the time, and her troops had quickly been put into Deep Sleep, so information about Jace might not have gotten through to her.

Carina recalled a second person she hadn't had anything to do with for a while: Calvaley. Had the old man been taken out of stasis? And if he had, where were they keeping him?

Mezban's guards had returned her to the *Bathsheba's* gym. When she entered the room for the second time, the lights were half their usual brightness. The place was also cooler than it had been. The soldiers had insisted she went with them immediately and didn't give her time to change out of her thin pajamas. She was also barefoot, as the closets in the suite held no shoes.

As soon as she stepped over the threshold cold air hit her, and she began to shiver.

Four Regians crouched at the far end of the gym, their black, spindly forms ill-defined in the shadows. Even if Carina hadn't seen one of the creatures a couple of days previously, she didn't need a closer look at the four in the gym to know their exact appearance. It had been etched on her mind for the last ten years: they were roughly as tall as a male human, but two-thirds of their height was in their three pairs of legs. Their upper third was as long as a man was tall, and narrow, like an upturned canoe, with a ridge like a keel running from the front to the back. Several shiny black eyes were centered at the thickened front end of the ridge, and two pairs of sharp mouth parts overlapped beneath the eyes.

She'd always had an interest in bugs, from as far back as she could remember, and she liked them all—except these ones.

At the mere sight of the Regians, her pulse sped up. Images from the attack on her settlement when she was a child flashed unbidden into her mind: one of the creatures trying to separate a father from his baby son, then changing its mind and lifting both on the dark carapace of its back; Saul, one of her several bullies, ripped from her grasp by black pincers; Nai Nai, looking up in terror when a Regian discovered her hiding place.

She swallowed and walked forward.

Along with the rest of the population where she'd grown up, she'd never known exactly what the creatures did with the victims they captured during their raids, except that the men, women, and children never came back.

She didn't want to find out, either, but it was looking inevitable.

Mezban stood with her husband near the door where Carina had entered. They were the only other humans in the room. The soldiers had silently withdrawn.

Lomang beckoned her over.

The man's demeanor had changed since she'd last seen him. It was clear his and Mezban's previous haughty attitude had been a show. Now, the man's eyes were wide with fear and his skin glistened with sweat.

"I know what you're going to say," said Carina before the smuggler had a chance to speak.

She could see he was holding a flask, no doubt full of elixir brewed by one of the children.

"You want me to impress our captors with a performance and save your miserable lives," she went on.

"It would be in your interest to do what we ask," Mezban said. "We know more about these creatures than you do. Our people have suffered their raids for thousands of years. We have information that could make your family's experience under their captivity more endurable."

Carina held out her hand for the elixir. As Lomang handed it over, she said to Mezban, "You would say that, wouldn't you? Why should I believe you? And even if you are speaking the truth, you're assuming the Regians are new to me. They aren't. My home planet borders the galactic desert we crossed to get to your sector, and my settlement was raided once."

She didn't mention that, as a child, she'd single-handedly driven the raiders away. She didn't want Lomang or Mezban to know any more than she'd just told them.

Mezban frowned. "And why should *we* believe *you*?"

"I don't give a shit whether you believe me. On the other hand, you'd better hope you have something genuine to offer."

At the corner of the hall, the four Regians stirred, shifting their monstrous, spindly legs, their pincers scraping on the hard floor.

Lomang's eyes grew wider. "They're growing impatient. Do something, quickly!"

Carina guessed the pair were down to their final chance

with the evil aliens. If she failed to Cast, would Lomang and Mezban become lunch? She smiled, enjoying their torment. Now that she had elixir, she could Transport out of there if the Regians attacked. There was a *lot* she could do with elixir in her hand. But to get everyone else who *deserved* saving out of there —not including the two who stood before her—would require planning and time.

"Why are you smiling?" Lomang demanded. "Don't you have any idea what those creatures can do?"

"To be honest, I don't have a clear picture," Carina said, "but I'd be interested to find out."

"P-please!" Lomang begged. "You must do something!"

To Mezban's credit, she didn't debase herself as her husband did. She only stiffened, and her gaze flicked repeatedly to the four creatures in the corner.

"You know," said Carina bitterly, "I might have been more inclined to help you if you hadn't murdered Cadwallader. That really was unforgivable."

"What did you expect us to do?" Mezban spat. "He was your leader. If he'd lived his soldiers would have rallied to him. He would have been a constant thorn in our side."

"And you think I won't?" Carina asked. "That is, assuming you survive the next five minutes."

"Stars, if I could bring him back I would," said Lomang. "I didn't know he meant so much to you. As my wife says, it was a logical, strategic decision. You would have done the same yourself. You *have* done the same."

He was referring to the execution of Sable Dirksen. But that hadn't been strategic. It had been a spur-of-the-moment action borne of rage and the desire for revenge.

"And yet," said Carina scathingly, "we didn't kill *you,* or *you.*" She pointed at the man and woman in turn.

Her statement was beyond denying. Lomang's lips folded over his large teeth like a trap.

The movements of the Regians became more agitated. A noise like a mixture between a hiss and a rattle sounded from their part of the gym.

She estimated the smuggler and Mezban's time was nearly up. "You have one chance to save yourselves. There were others you took out of stasis who were especially important to me. If they live, I'll do a little performance, then we'll talk about what happens going forward. If you killed any of these three people, you'll follow them, courtesy of our friends over there. You can lie, of course, but that'll only delay your deaths for as long as it takes me to find out."

"We didn't kill anyone else!" Lomang spluttered. "Only your commander. That's right, isn't it, Mezban, my love?"

She held Carina's gaze with her own, her eyes hooded. "My husband speaks the truth. Only the blue-eyed man died."

Carina turned her attention to Lomang.

"Actually, that isn't quite correct," he said, under her stare.

"What?" Mezban also glared at him.

"My love," he said nervously, "Some of the mercenaries died when the ship was taken by the Regians. Do you remember? We found their bodies and put them in the airlock."

"Ah yes." Mezban's gaze moved to Carina. "But *we* did not kill them. And if you're worried about the old man, he remains in stasis. The Regians told us they don't want his aged body."

"Calvaley?" she asked.

"If that is his name," Mezban replied disdainfully. "I never inquired."

Carina decided to take their words, for now.

One of the aliens lifted itself up, and began to walk toward them. The hissing rattle grew louder. It was clearly this one that was talking.

"One more thing," said Carina.

"Yes!" squeaked Lomang. "What? Anything!"

"My siblings and I are to be released from captivity immediately. We are to have the freedom of the ship."

From the corner of her eye, Carina saw Mezban give a small smirk, which the woman hastily shut down when Carina turned to look at her.

"Yes, we agree!" Lomang exclaimed.

The Regian was halfway across the gym. Its mouth parts were opening and closing, perhaps because it was speaking or perhaps because it was anticipating a tasty meal.

Carina opened the flask. It contained only one mouthful of elixir, not enough to do anything major. She would have dearly loved to space Lomang and Mezban, but she had to be cautious. She swigged the elixir, then closed her eyes and swiftly Cast. When she opened her eyes, Lomang was already moving through the air.

She'd contemplated sending him in the direction of the approaching Regian, but if he opened his bowels in fear that could be messy. Instead, she sent him in the opposite direction. When he neared the gym wall, she dropped him, heavily enough to make a satisfying *thump*, but not break his bones.

The Regian paused, its pincers clicking on the floor, as if in thought.

Over the next few minutes, the reason for Mezban's ill-concealed smirk became clear.

After dumping Lomang on the other side of the gym, Carina noticed a slim, rectangular bump on Mezban's chest, under her clothing. She'd thought Mezban and Lomang understood the Regians' language, but when she saw the bump, she suspected this wasn't the case.

She stepped up to Mezban and reached into the neck of her shirt.

"Hey!" the woman protested, trying to fight her off.

But Carina was too fast. She felt for a string, located it, and yanked it. A translator emerged from Mezban's shirt. Carina pulled it over her head and at the same time she thrust an open hand toward the woman. "Give me your comm," she demanded.

Mezban popped the small device out of her ear and handed it over, sending Carina a black look along with it.

Wrinkling her nose, she wiped the comm on her pajama pants before inserting it into her own ear.

Immediately, she heard a long string of words in Universal Speech, even though she could hear nothing inside the room. The Regians were talking to each other, but she guessed the pitch of their voices was mostly outside the normal human hearing range. The noises she'd heard them making before had only been a small part of what they'd been saying.

However, the translator she now held in her hand wasn't effective at translating the creatures' language. She frowned, trying to make sense of what she was hearing.

The four Regians seemed to be arguing. She heard *Humans* and *No* a lot, as well as *Better way* and *Prefer*. She also heard *Soon*, *Decide now*, and *No, later*.

The aliens constantly talked over each other. They understood what was being said, no doubt, but from a human perspective the conversation was one big jumble. Also, the translator didn't convey any differences in the individuals' voice. They all sounded exactly alike, so it was impossible to focus on one of them to try to comprehend what it was saying.

Carina closed her eyes in an effort to comprehend the gist at least.

She heard *Arrive soon* a bunch of times, and *No time left*.

Her heart sank as she realized what she was probably hearing, and why Mezban had smirked at her demand for the freedom of the ship: the *Bathsheba* had nearly arrived at her destination. The amount of time Carina and her siblings had to enjoy that freedom was limited. They could be down to a mere few hours for moving around the vessel, communicating with their friends and allies, and devising a plan to defeat the Regians.

She opened her eyes and asked Mezban, "How long do we have before we reach their planet?"

"We aren't sure exactly."

Carina grew angry. First the smirk, and now Mezban was apparently being deliberately vague. She was as much of an idiot as her husband. If they were to survive, they needed Carina. They should be helping her, not making everything more difficult.

Her anger must have shown because the woman held up her hands.

"Honestly, we don't know. But it isn't long."

"So that's why they told you to get everyone out of stasis. They wanted us all ready to disembark. And what's going to happen when we arrive?"

Lomang had gotten up and was walking toward them, limping and grimacing.

The small woman's face was gloomy. "That's what you were helping us with. We have very little information on what happens to people captured by Regians, and what we do have has come from secondhand sources. It's said that they prize human meat as a food, but they also use us as slaves on their farms. We were hoping that your skills would be useful for the latter function, and we wanted to find out all that mages can do so we would have some roles to suggest to our captors."

"Human slaves for agriculture? Why would they need us for that? Machinery is way more efficient."

Mezban shrugged. "Who knows? But I would say it's preferable to being eaten."

"Most things are," said Lomang.

He'd arrived while the women had been speaking.

Carina came to a decision.

"I'm leaving," she said, then, glancing at the Regians, who

still seemed to be arguing about what to do, she added, "providing these creatures let me."

"I doubt they'll try to stop you," said Mezban. "Everywhere except the residential areas is sealed off. They've allowed us free run of those areas, knowing we can't escape."

"I want to know one more thing," Carina said. "How long was I in stasis? Wait. Two things. Has the *Bathsheba* been diverted far from her original course?"

Lomang answered: "All we know is the Regians deactivated our stasis capsules six weeks ago. Your Deep Sleep chamber was sealed off, but then they told us to wake you all in stages over the next few weeks."

"It was then we realized our chance," said Mezban. "We thought, the mages can deliver us. But your siblings were not capable of demonstrating their talents to our captors. You, on the other hand, have the opportunity to save us. You must take it. You must…"

Indignation and fury blazed in Carina. She stepped up to the woman and glared down into her little, smug face. "*You* had the opportunity to save *one* man's life! Not even that—you had the chance to simply allow him to live, and you didn't take it. Why the hell should I save you?"

Lomang spluttered, "But you said—"

Carina was already leaving.

24

Parthenia paced the floor of the living room, rigid with outrage.

"How could they have been so stupid!" she exclaimed.

"I know, I know," said Carina, rubbing a spot between her eyebrows.

She was half-sitting, half-lying on the sofa. Her eyes were sunken in shadows and her skin was pale and tight. She was experiencing the effects of her time in stasis. Parthenia had been similarly affected, and so had their siblings. Carina would recover in a few days, but from what Mezban had said, they didn't have that long. They had only hours to act, and it was all due to Lomang and Mezban's idiocy.

"If they'd given us our freedom..." Parthenia went on. "If they'd taken you out of stasis earlier...We would have figured out a way to take back control of the ship by now. We would have spaced the Regians and continued to Earth."

Carina groaned and sat up, resting her elbows on her knees and letting her head flop down.

"But instead they wanted to retain control over us," said

Parthenia. "They chose to *use* us to try to impress the Regians when we could have entirely defeated them. Only that would have left Lomang and Mezban beholden to us. They *had* to be in charge, even as we're all being transported to our deaths."

"Or to be used as slave labor on farms," Carina reminded her.

"Yeah..." Parthenia paused, then said, "That part doesn't make any sense."

"Right. It doesn't. But that's the least of our worries. I... Ugh...I think I'm gonna be sick." Carina got up and ran to the bathroom.

Parthenia sat down and tried to ignore the sound of her sister vomiting, or, rather, retching. As far as she knew, she hadn't eaten a thing since coming out of Deep Sleep.

It was clear Carina needed her help, and, from what she'd said about them working together, it sounded like this time she might actually accept it.

The thought brought a small spark of joy, despite the dangers they faced. But she didn't really believe her sister would ever give up trying to control her or their brothers and sisters.

That was a problem for later, however. What should they do first?

One step was obvious: they had to make more elixir. But then what?

Carina emerged from the bathroom, wiping her mouth. She flopped down onto the sofa, asking, "I look like shit, don't I?"

"You've looked better."

Suddenly Parthenia knew she'd never stopped loving her sister, in spite of everything that had happened between them, yet, somehow, she *liked* her better when she was weak and vulnerable.

"I can barely think," Carina said. "We should do something —now. But I'm not sure what. Maybe we should focus on finding Jace. The Regians know I can Cast, and they know you all can too. That's what Lomang told them even though they didn't see a demonstration. So they'll be wary of all of us. They're probably already figuring out the possibilities of what we can do. But I don't think they know about Jace."

A door to one of the bedrooms opened, and a tousle-haired Ferne poked his head out.

"You two are up early."

"You don't know the half of it," Parthenia replied. "Wake up Oriana. I want you both to make some more elixir, fast."

"But—"

"We're allowed out of the suite," she interrupted. "Hurry up."

He darted across the living room to another door.

"Nahla will get woken up, too," said Parthenia, "but that can't be helped."

"She needs to be awake and alert," Carina said. "She also has to stick close by us while we do whatever it is we're going to do. The Regians believe she's a mage, and they might hurt her if she doesn't Cast for them."

"I'll tell her when she's up. I was thinking, if we're fast and we all Cast together, we could simply Transport all the Regians outside the ship. Then the *Bathsheba's* ours."

"It isn't going to be that easy," replied Carina. "We don't know how many there are or where they're situated. Mezban said all the operational areas of the ship are sealed off. I'm guessing that's where most of the Regians are right now. And they came here in their own ship, don't forget. That must be following alongside us or joined to our ship like the *Duchess* and the *Peregrine,* and it'll be carrying a crew." She shook her head. "There's going to be a battle. No doubt about it. I hope the Black Dogs' weapons haven't been destroyed. We need to find them."

Ferne emerged from the bedroom, followed by Oriana, sleepy-eyed.

"Can we really go outside now?" she asked.

"Yes," Parthenia replied, "but be careful."

"I don't think Lomang and Mezban are going to give up control easily," said Carina. "They might try something—perhaps try to force you to Cast for them, or use you as hostages. It would be stupid of them, of course, but they've shown a special talent for that."

"Don't worry," Ferne said airily. "It won't take us long to make more elixir. As soon as we have it, if Lomang comes near us I'll threaten to Cast Fire into his hat."

Oriana chuckled.

"This isn't the time for joking," Parthenia said sternly.

As they'd been talking, Ferne and Oriana had crossed the living room to the main door.

Ferne opened it and peered outside. "The guards have gone."

They went outside, but before Ferne left he looked back at Parthenia and Carina. "I'm glad you've kissed and made up. Everything's *so much* nicer when you act maturely."

The door closed.

Carina raised her eyebrows. "Did he mean me?"

"I think he meant both of us," Parthenia replied.

HALF AN HOUR LATER, the mages, armed with still-hot elixir, were roaming the *Bathsheba*, searching for the Black Dogs. They walked the empty, silent corridors as a group. Carina hadn't wanted to split up for the search and Parthenia had agreed with her. Despite the greater efficiency, the younger children could be taken hostage, especially Nahla, who had no way of defending herself.

They were at the highest level, where many suites were situated, but they found them all unlocked and unoccupied. Lomang and Mezban had apparently wanted to keep them separated from those who might help them.

They turned a corner, and were suddenly confronted by a solid metal wall that blocked the route entirely. The Regians had sealed it off.

"What's through there?" Oriana asked.

"The viewing dome," replied Carina.

"Why don't the Regians want us to go to that?" asked Ferne.

"No idea. We'll have to go back the way we came. Try another direction." The elevators weren't working, so they found an access shaft and climbed down it to the next level.

Here, things were busier. They passed several of Mezban's troops, but without incident. The soldiers had clearly been told to leave them alone.

But they still couldn't find the mercs.

"We should just ask one of them," said Parthenia.

"Or I'll Enthrall someone," Oriana offered.

"Yes," Carina said. She about-faced and ran back to the last person they'd passed—an older man, who looked as though his years in the military had been long and hard.

"Where are the Black Dogs?" she demanded. "Where are you keeping them?" Her hand moved toward the canister of elixir on her hip.

The man's features signaled his alarm. "There's no need for that, miss! The mercs are being held in the refectory. Just along there aways." He pointed in the direction they'd already been heading.

Carina turned and ran back to her siblings, but she didn't stop. She sped right past them, calling out, "Come on. We don't know how much time we have."

Outside the refectory, a group of ten or more of Mezban's men and women stood, but they were unarmed.

"Move aside," Carina ordered.

The troops parted silently, watching the mages. Parthenia stepped through them and tried the door.

"It's locked," she told the others.

That made sense: lacking armed troops, Lomang and Mezban had put the mercs in the refectory while they were still groggy from stasis and unable to put up much of a fight, and then simply sealed them in. They would have access to food and restrooms in there, though little else.

Carina was already Casting Unlock.

A moment later, she opened the door wide, and the smell of unwashed bodies floated out.

"Phooey!" exclaimed Oriana, wafting the space in front of her nose.

"It's Lin and the kids!" someone inside the refectory shouted.

Whoops and hollers followed.

Carina went inside, and Parthenia peeked in.

Immediately, she covered her mouth and chuckled.

Mezban's guards hadn't given the mercs anything to wear after taking them from their Deep Sleep capsules, and the men and women had improvised by creating underwear from table napkins. They resembled large, muscly babies, naked except for their diapers.

Several of the Black Dogs had descended on Carina and were alternately slapping her back and lifting her off the floor in bear hugs. Over the sound of cheers and yells of general jubilation, Parthenia could faintly hear her sister protesting and telling them to be quiet.

Then through the hubbub she heard someone call her name.

She turned.

Kamil.

Tears suddenly welling up from nowhere, she ran up to him and threw her arms around him.

"Hey, you probably don't want to do that," he said, half-heartedly. "I must stink."

"I don't care."

She hugged him tighter. "I didn't know if you'd made it. I thought you might have been killed when the Regians took the ship."

"No, I missed out on that battle."

"Thank the stars you did."

Kamil pulled away from her to look her in the eyes.

"I was lucky in another way," he said. "I hoped you were too precious to be killed, and I was right."

25

Mezban's troops could have been a useful ally in their effort to defeat the Regians and escape aboard the *Bathsheba*, but Carina didn't trust them. As soon as she could be heard above the noise of celebration, she'd ordered the Black Dogs to round up every man and woman they could find who wasn't a member of their band, and lock them in the refectory.

Lomang, Mezban, and Pappu were found hiding in the closet of one of the largest suites. They joined their troops, after Carina had relieved Lomang of his translator and comm and given them to Parthenia.

No Regians had been found in the section of the ship where they'd confined the humans. No doubt they had lockable entrances to the area as well as the solid steel walls, but she wasn't going to try to find them. The portals would be exactly the places the Regians would be expecting them to try to force entry.

She had a better idea.

"I don't like this, Car," said Atoi as they stood next to one of the metal seals the aliens had created. "It'd be better for us all to face them head on, full force. If you two go in, working alone..."

"Have you ever been in a firefight with Regians?" asked Carina.

"No, but—"

"This is the best way, believe me. And when we get the rifles to you, remind everyone what I said. Long bursts of fire."

Bryce was also there.

Carina had been overjoyed to discover he was among the mercs in the refectory, but their time for catching up had been fleeting. She turned to take a look at him one last time, just in case she never saw him again.

"I know you know what you're doing better than any of us," he said, "but take care."

"You too."

"Ready?" asked Parthenia.

She nodded. "Let's go."

Together, they took a drink of elixir from their flasks.

Carina closed her eyes, Cast, and then opened them again.

Cold, humid air enveloped her. The armory Cadwallader had created, which lay on the Regian-occupied side of the *Bathsheba*, was in complete darkness.

"Phew!" Parthenia whispered. "No one's around."

It was as Carina had expected. The aliens hadn't seen any reason to post guards *inside* the weapon store. Her demonstration in the gym didn't seem to have given the creatures too much of an indication of what mages could do.

She Cast Fire onto one of the rolled-up napkins she'd brought along. It blazed up, and the flames' light reflected from the muzzles of the pulse rifles surrounding them. One-handed, she grabbed one for herself and gave another to Parthenia.

"If we're disturbed, remember to do what I said," she told her. "I know you hate it. I do, too, but nothing else works as well." Seeing a glint of defiance appear in Parthenia's eyes, she added, "I'm not trying to boss you around. It's the truth. Now, hurry. We don't have long."

They began to Transport the weapons to the mercs waiting on the other side of the ship. Carina sent one row, then Parthenia Transported the row beneath it.

A loud, ululating whine sounded. The fire alarm.

"Quick," Carina urged, "it'll take them a moment to find out the location of the fire."

They managed to Transport two more rows of rifles before the door opened.

Instantly, Carina dropped the burning napkins and stamped out the flames.

"Now us," she breathed to her sister, "but let me do it."

A hulking figure blocked the dim light entering from the passage. Carina prepared to Cast and grabbed her sister's hand. The Regian's body swayed as it looked—or perhaps smelled—for them. Abruptly, it halted.

Then it sprang.

Before it reached them, they'd left the armory and appeared on one side of a metal seal—the Regian side. At the far end of the corridor stood the entrance to the viewing dome.

The lighting was dim as twilight under a cloudy sky. On the other side of the steel sheet, Atoi and the rest of the Black Dogs would be arming themselves with the newly arrived weapons, but Carina and her sister still had plenty to do.

Suddenly, Parthenia's hand fastened on her arm. Her sister had frozen, staring into the darkness.

Then Carina saw it: a single Regian, far down the passageway, facing away from them.

"We'll never get past it without it seeing us," she said softly.

"Do we need to?" asked Parthenia.

"Yes. I don't want to Transport directly into the dome. If my guess is right, we could be dead before we know it."

"So what do we do?"

"Get rid of it before it sees us."

Parthenia made an anguished face. She averted her gaze, and her grip on Carina's arm became painfully tight. "Do it, then."

Carina made the hated Cast.

When she opened her eyes, in the low light she thought she saw a fissure open in the Regian's back. Instantly a whistle-like shriek, picked up by the translator around her neck, was transmitted to her comm. The noise pierced Carina's ear and she grimaced in pain.

Parthenia winced and held a hand to the side of her head.

The fissure in the creature opened wider. It gaped, and powder issued from the gap, creating a dark cloud that dimmed the light further. The creature's legs buckled and it collapsed, but before it hit the ground, it was gone.

Parthenia had watched the Regian's last moments out of the corners of her eyes. As it disappeared, she gasped.

"I know," Carina murmured. "I can't explain it. Now we have to—"

The doors to the viewing dome flew open, and aliens tumbled out. A river of the black creatures flowed from the doorway.

Carina gaped. She'd guessed they would see some Regians as they tried to carry out her plan, but she hadn't imagined so many had descended upon the *Bathsheba*. It was like an infestation.

"You were right!" Parthenia quietly exclaimed.

Carina was already swallowing elixir. It was time to go to their next stop.

MEZBAN'S BOMB was exactly where Rosa, the person who had disarmed it, had said she'd left it: in the *Duchess's* armory. She'd said she'd *thought it might come in useful one day*, and so she'd put it on the mercs' ship for safekeeping. How lucky they were she had.

Understanding how to arm the device and set it to explode without the object in front of her or reference had been tricky, but Carina had thought she understood. Now her memory was to be put to the test.

Parthenia hovered at the armory door in the silent, dark vessel, keeping watch. The Regians had possibly sealed it off from the *Bathsheba*, thinking they would foil an escape attempt, but that was no impediment to mages.

It was a damned shame they'd alerted the aliens to their presence so early, firstly by setting off the fire alarm and, secondly, by killing the Regian outside the viewing dome. By now, the creatures had probably entered the section where they'd confined the humans and were engaged in battle with the mercs.

Carina had to act fast. She opened the device's casing and searched for the components Rosa had described. She halted, confused.

"Have you done it?" asked Parthenia.

"No, not yet." Carina peered into the bomb's interior. Her mind had gone a blank. She kept thinking of Darius, Nahla, Oriana, and Ferne, helping the Black Dogs battle the Regians, Casting the abhorrent Split. It was the only sure way to kill the aliens, but it was a horrible thing for a mage to do. Jace had balked at even the suggestion until Carina had explained the need.

She didn't know if the mage would do it, but at least he would be there to protect the kids.

Her thoughts were also consumed with fear for Bryce. He had nothing to defend himself with except a rifle.

The people she loved were in dire danger, and she couldn't help feeling that, again, it was her fault.

"Carina!" Parthenia barked. "Have you *done* it?"

She looked at her sister helplessly. "I..."

"Let me arm it," said Parthenia, striding over.

"No, it's okay. I can manage." She stared down into the device.

"Give it to me."

Carina looked at her sister's outstretched hands and back at the bomb. "No, it's fine. I think I remember now."

"Will you for *once* in your life let someone else take control?!" Parthenia yelled.

Carina sighed, crushed by the truth of the words. Wordlessly, she lifted the object in her hands and passed it to her sister.

Parthenia frowned as she focused on the wires and relays. Deftly, she reached in and made some adjustments. "It's armed." She picked up the detonator. "Back to the viewing dome, right?"

"Yeah," Carina replied, deflated. "Back to the dome."

SHE'D SUSPECTED the corridor leading to the viewing dome had been sealed off because the Regians were using it for something. For what, she had no idea. But there was nothing else of importance in that part of the ship, no access to the *Bathsheba's* controls or anything useful, so the place the aliens wanted the humans cut off from was the dome itself.

That was why she'd wanted to check it out before going there with the bomb.

As it turned out, the decision had worked in their favor. When they reappeared in the corridor outside the dome, the place seemed empty. The door stood open, and the area was silent. The Regians had been drawn away by the disturbance Carina and Parthenia had created.

"Let's get in there, fast," said Carina, "before they come back."

The two women raced down the passage toward the room. As they darted inside, however, Parthenia squeaked and drew back. Three of the aliens remained inside. Carina caught a glimpse of lines of swollen, square objects hanging from the struts across the ceiling before she dashed out of the room. They ran back to the steel wall.

Carina's hand moved to the flask at her hip, but Parthenia stopped her.

Breathless and wide-eyed, she said, "No, I'll do it."

The monsters emerged from the room.

Carina cursed and lifted the rifle swinging from her shoulder.

Parthenia's canister was already open and its mouth at her lips.

The Regians sped toward them, their long bodies rising up on their nimble limbs.

Carina fired, but the aliens had already moved into time-shift mode. Their figures blurred in the dim light. She held down the trigger, spraying a rapid stream of pulses in an arc across the corridor.

Beside her, her sister's eyes were closed.

Carina hoped to hell she didn't hesitate. Split was a Cast that was never supposed to be used on living things, and it was how their mother had killed Parthenia's father after her sister had unknowingly given her the elixir to do it. Could she overcome her mental barrier?

One of the pulses hit its mark, and an oncoming Regian burst into flaming dust. The other two were nearly upon them.

A jet of liquid burst from a hole in the front carapace of one of the creatures.

"Parthenia!" Carina heard the fear in her own voice.

The liquid splashed onto her sister.

Parthenia screamed.

Her shrill wail was joined by shrieks from Carina's comm.

Just before they reached the women, the Regians fell forward onto their crumpling front limbs, spurted black powder, and vanished.

Parthenia was still shrieking, her hands raised, fingers splayed, and her mouth an agonized O.

A line of open, bloody, weeping flesh ran down her cheek and neck and scored a groove in her top and the skin underneath. The alien had sprayed her with acid.

Trembling with shock, Carina reached for her elixir. After swallowing a mouthful, she wrote the Heal Character and sent it out to her sister, but all the while she was fighting flashbacks of doing the same for Darius on Ostillon after Sable Dirksen had shot him.

Parthenia's screaming stopped.

Carina opened her eyes. Her sister's skin was whole and healthy, the wound from the acid entirely gone.

"Thanks," said Parthenia.

But Carina couldn't speak. She was breathing too fast, and her chest felt like it was about to explode.

She hadn't known the Regians had that capability. She couldn't shake the image of her sister's injury from her mind, and she was imagining what could be happening to the mercs on the other side of the ship.

What if they'd sprayed Bryce? What if they'd gotten through the soldiers who were defending the kids?

Parthenia grabbed her shoulders and shook her. "It's okay! I'm *okay*. Come on, we have to set the bomb."

26

Perhaps because they'd been unable to locate the humans who had infiltrated their section of the *Bathsheba*, the Regians seemed to have focused their efforts on attacking the ones they could reach. When Carina returned with her sister to the mercs' side of the vessel, it was thick with aliens, and more were flowing into the area, she saw with dismay.

The black, ridged backs were everywhere, blurring in and out of focus, and she could smell the terrible odor of burned human flesh. The creatures had been spraying the soldiers with acid. Had they been wearing armor, the effect wouldn't have been devastating, but the Black Dogs were nearly naked.

Carina and Parthenia were near the gym, where Carina had told Atoi to shelter if the Regians showed up.

"What now?" asked Parthenia.

They had seconds before the aliens noticed them.

A hum of words streamed from Carina's comm: *Kill! Destroy! Eat! Execute! Infest! Massacre! Slay!* She could also hear the shriek of aliens being Split.

The rustling of many shell-covered bodies moving and

scraping against each other filled her other ear along with the hissing rattle of their speech that was audible to human hearing.

Suddenly, an awful cry broke through the cacophony. Someone had been hit with the corrosive liquid.

"Transport us in there," she said, nodding at the entrance to the gym, which teemed with black carapaces.

While Parthenia prepared to Cast, she plucked the detonator out of her sister's hands and pressed the switch.

A beat later, a dull, concussive *Boom!* sounded, and a shockwave passed through the floor.

As one, the milling Regians froze and their rustling stilled to silence.

The next thing Carina knew, she was inside the gym.

Parthenia had Transported them to the side farthest away from the entrance where the Regians were massed. The mercs held most of the gym floor, pressing the black bugs into one corner of the room, but the Black Dogs were in a bad way. Horrific burns had incapacitated many of them, and the line holding back the encroaching aliens looked dangerously thin.

She saw Bryce down, his legs burned, but she had no time to go to him.

Jace and Darius were Healing the injured men and women, Nahla was giving them water, and Oriana and Ferne appeared to have been concentrating on Splitting the Regians. Entire sections of the creatures were regularly dissolving into black dust that vanished, but the quantity of them swarming outside the gym told Carina the mercs and mages were fighting a losing battle. She'd wondered how the aliens had managed to take the *Bathsheba* in the first place, but now the answer was clear: they'd simply overwhelmed the Black Dogs' defense with sheer weight of numbers.

The creatures' stillness as they reacted to the explosion

abruptly broke. Some of those in the gym sped away, but others remained and continued their attack.

"Car!" yelled Atoi, noticing her arrival. "That was the bomb, right?"

"Yeah."

On the Regian-held side of the *Bathsheba*, depressurization was taking place. Carina and Parthenia had Cast Open on the door to the viewing dome and on the access hatches to the lower decks. No matter what the aliens did, they would not be able to close the doors for ten or fifteen minutes at least, by which time the damage would be done. Atmosphere was flying out of the ship into space, taking aliens with it as well as anything else not fixed down. It would be mayhem.

Carina's plan had been to get rid of most of the enemy this way rather than through a direct attack. It had seemed the best tactic for regaining control of the colony ship with minimal human casualties—the metal seals would prevent the depressurization extending to their section. Sending the pulse rifles to the mercs had only been a precaution.

But things hadn't gone according to plan. She'd anticipated the viewing dome might be filled with aliens, but she'd underestimated the sheer amount of them, and she hadn't imagined so many would move to the other side of the ship to attack their prisoners. Now the aliens were also protected by the seals.

The Black Dogs were facing an insurmountable enemy. The Regians' time-shifting made them hard to kill with pulse fire, and without armor the mercs were helpless before the aliens' acid attacks, while the mages' powers weren't sufficient to tip the balance. Two mages' efforts had been taken up with Healing the soldiers' burns, halving their offensive capability. And their supply of elixir was finite.

Even now that she and Parthenia had returned, things looked bad.

While Carina had been brooding, Parthenia had begun to

help with the Healing, and Atoi had returned her attention to the firefight.

She called her old friend's name.

"What?" Atoi yelled in reply. As she spoke, she turned toward Carina, revealing a bright red splash of acid burn down her right-hand side.

"It's not going to work," Carina shouted. "We can't retake the *Bathsheba*."

"Right," said Atoi, digesting the fact. "Got any other ideas?"

"Yep. Plan B."

"You have a plan B?"

"I just thought of it. Hold the line as long as you can."

"Sure," Atoi replied, hefting her rifle to her shoulder and spraying out a long burst of pulse fire. "I was gonna send everyone on R&R, but we'll stick around."

Carina ran to Darius, who was kneeling next to a woman who had been so badly burned the white of her rib bones showed through the damaged flesh. Her little brother's face was pale and wretched. He'd seen too much death and pain in his short life.

After she told him what she needed him to do, he nodded gravely and said, "I'll fix this lady first, okay?"

"Okay, sweetheart," Carina replied. Then she ran to speak to her other siblings and, lastly, to Jace.

The mages began work.

Groups of the worst-injured mercs disappeared first, followed by the walking wounded.

When the area behind the fighting men and women was empty, Carina told Ferne, Oriana, and Darius to Transport themselves and Nahla next.

"No!" Oriana protested. "I want to—"

"Leave!" Carina hollered.

Then she saw Parthenia giving her the stink eye.

"Go," she said, more quietly. "Please."

"Hmpf." Oriana turned to her brothers. "Let's get out of here."

A few moments later, the three children disappeared.

With the younger ones out of the way, Carina could concentrate on Transporting the remaining mercs strategically to ensure the fewest casualties. Some of them were going to get hurt—it was unavoidable. As their numbers decreased the Regians would push forward, and the last remaining group would be overrun.

Scanning the battle scene, she pointed out sections of fighting men and women to Jace and Parthenia. She didn't Transport any herself, wanting to concentrate on the firefight.

When the mercs she'd indicated had vanished, the Regians quickly moved in. The scrape and rattle of alien hides rubbing together and their murderous words in her comm grew louder.

"You two now," she yelled to Parthenia and Jace.

Parthenia nodded gravely before taking a drink of elixir.

But Jace didn't. He touched Carina's arm. "Together," he mouthed.

She had no time to argue.

The aliens were crushing inward. A long scream rent the air. A merc was down.

Carina lifted her canister of elixir to her lips and tipped it up.

A scant few drops dribbled into her mouth.

Empty!

She'd used it all.

Another cry of agony came from the remaining soldiers.

Blurring black shapes loomed large in her vision.

Then she was gone.

27

Arms gripped her tightly around her waist and a small head buried itself in her stomach.

"I thought you were gonna die!" Darius exclaimed, his voice muffled.

"No, I'm still here." Carina put her hand on her brother's head, her heart thumping wildly from her narrow escape. "Don't worry, I'm still alive—just." She turned to Jace, who stood nearby on *Duchess's* bridge. If it hadn't been for his decision to stay with her until the last moment, she and the last few mercs to be Transported would have died. "Thanks. I don't know how I—"

He raised a hand to stop her. "A simple thanks is enough. But next time, remember what happened a moment ago. Accept the help that's offered to you. If we all insisted on tackling our problems alone, none of us would succeed. We need each other."

She nodded, took in a deep breath, and exhaled. "Okay, I hear you." She scanned the bridge.

Parthenia and Ferne were Healing the recently arrived

mercs, other soldiers were leaving, on their way to their stations. Bryce and Atoi were nowhere to be seen. Oriana was lifting Nahla into a seat. Hsiao was already at the flight controls.

"We need to get this ship moving," Carina said.

"I'm detaching us from the *Bathsheba*," said Hsiao. "Everyone, strap in." The pilot sent the same message over the ship's comm.

Carina picked up Darius and thrust him into a seat, then took the next nearest empty seat.

"Where's Bryce?" she asked generally as her seat's safety harness slid out and over her before automatically snapping closed.

"He's okay," said Parthenia. "I Healed him. But I'm all out of elixir. I need to make some more."

"No time," said Carina.

"*Everyone* strap in," Hsiao repeated, louder.

The pilot didn't need telling that they had to make a quick getaway before the Regians realized where they'd gone. The *Bathsheba* was too large and cumbersome to catch the *Duchess*, and her weaponry was mostly defensive, but the aliens must have arrived in another ship of their own. *That* vessel was an unknown quantity.

A jerk signaled the decoupling of the *Duchess* from the colony ship.

Hsiao began to bring her about.

Carina hoped the Regians had already discovered Mezban, Lomang, and the rest of the people in the refectory, and so they wouldn't bother coming after the mercs. She felt bad about consigning Mezban's troops a nasty fate, but she couldn't save everyone. As for Mezban, Lomang, and Pappu, she didn't spare them a second thought.

"Brace for acceleration," Hsiao warned.

The *Duchess* slammed forward.

Carina grasped the arms of her seat as the Gs hit, focusing on keeping her breathing shallow and fast.

The interface screen to her left displayed a scanner-derived image of the surrounding space. On it, she saw the asymmetrical bulk of the *Bathsheba*, and, protruding from one of the colony ship's sides, the much smaller *Peregrine*.

She cursed, realizing her mistake.

The *Duchess* had seemed the obvious vessel to take. She'd been a home to Carina for a long time, even before she'd found her family, and when she'd returned to her to retrieve the bomb, she been fairly certain no Regians were aboard. But the *Peregrine* was equipped with a particle beam and she was faster than the mercs' ship.

No point in wasting time on regrets. They'd taken the lesser ship, and that was that.

The Regians' vessel wasn't visible, probably due to being obscured by the vast *Bathsheba*. She hoped the *Duchess* was a match for the aliens' ship.

Hsiao was pulling them away at an almost-unendurable speed. Carina struggled to remain conscious. All the kids, including Parthenia, were out already, their heads lolling.

A minute passed, then two. She imagined the situation aboard the *Bathsheba*. The Regians would have registered the departure of the *Duchess* immediately. How would they react? Would they launch their own vessel? It would take them time to crew her and move her from the lee of the colony ship.

Carina reached out to the interface screen, fighting the acceleration force trying to pin her arm to her seat, and searched for nearby star systems. If the worse came to the worst and the Regians seemed about to recapture them, they might be able to escape to a planet.

A star system appeared, containing one habitable planet! The world's gravity was zero point five Standard, but that would only make things easier if they ended up in a survival situation.

Then she remembered an important point: the *Bathsheba* had nearly arrived at the Regians' intended destination.

Damn!

The planet she was looking at was one of their worlds, and going there would be a death sentence.

Something else caught her attention. Beyond the Regians' system an area of dark gray cloud hung in the void. The conglomeration of gases resembled a nebula, but it didn't look like any nebula she'd ever seen.

She switched the display to purely scan data, and blinked. The figures were going haywire. Some movement was to be expected due to the *Duchess's* increasing velocity, but the movement should have been steady and predictable. The data she was seeing was changing in a chaotic fashion. She couldn't make any sense of it, and realized the gray cloud shown on the interface display wasn't a representation of a known object, but an attempt to show something *unknown*.

In all the time she'd spent aboard starships, she'd never encountered something the computers couldn't identify.

But the strange phenomenon that lay outside the Regians' star system was the least of her worries. They might need a planetary escape route and none lay nearby. On the other hand, perhaps they wouldn't need a sanctuary. Several minutes had passed and there was no sign of pursuit. Were the Regians content with the humans still in their possession? She hardly dared hope it was true.

The colony ship was a lost cause, and without the Deep Sleep capsules the voyage to Earth would have to be postponed or even abandoned, but at least they would be safe.

"*Fuck!*" Hsiao exclaimed.

Carina took a moment to see what had alarmed the pilot, but when she did, her heart sank into her boots.

The *Peregrine* was pulling away from the *Bathsheba*. Who was flying her? It seemed weird the Regians would use an unfamiliar ship to try to catch them. Whatever the explanation, Mezban's destroyer was going to come after them, and, unless a miracle also came their way, they were screwed.

"What should I do?" Hsiao yelled, though the bridge was nearly silent save for the hum of the *Duchess's* engines.

Carina didn't know what to answer her. In situations like these, Cadwallader would be the one giving the orders. Atoi was next in command, but she wasn't on the bridge. And the weapons officer was also absent.

"Uh, just keep on doing what you're doing," she replied. Straining with effort, she touched the interface again, opening the *Duchess's* weapons system. She brought all the pulse cannons online and readied them.

"Do you know what *you're* doing?" asked Hsiao, squinting over her shoulder at Carina.

"Not exactly," she replied, "but I'm the best we've got right now."

Part of her interface screen displayed the scan data. The *Peregrine* was advancing on them at breathtaking speed. She wondered if the Regians' exoskeletons allowed them to endure more Gs than humans could.

She fixed her gaze on the data, her fingers hovering over the screen, waiting for the moment the destroyer came within range of the cannons. Their only hope was to take the ship out before its particle beam fired. The beam's range was shorter, but a direct hit would cripple or destroy the *Duchess*.

The numbers ticked down. A split second before they hit the cannons' effective range, Carina pressed down, firing them all at exactly the right moment. The screen tracked the pulses' silent progress across space. The *Peregrine* fired defensively, and its own pulses annihilated most of the *Duchess's* long before they reached their target. One got through, however, and impacted on the destroyer's hull, its energy splashing into space.

The hit was nowhere near enough to slow the *Peregrine's* onward progress. The ship flew on unaffected.

The *Duchess's* pulse cannons had powered up again. Carina fired, and again the bolts of pure energy sped across the void. The *Peregrine's* response was rapid and devastating. This time, none of the pulses made it through.

And all the while the distance between the two ships was closing.

Carina watched the readouts from the *Duchess's* cannons, willing them to operate faster, even though she knew it was hopeless, that the battle was already lost.

Then the thing she'd been dreading happened: the *Peregrine's* particle beam lanced out.

"*No!*" she whispered.

A beat later, she was thrown violently forward. The straps of her safety harness dug in painfully.

The merc vessel's acceleration had abruptly cut out. The hum of her engines had been silenced. An almost inaudible *click* sounded, and Carina gently floated up from her seat, restrained only by her harness.

"What's happened?" asked Parthenia groggily as she regained consciousness. "Did we get away? Oh!" She grabbed the straps holding her down.

"Gravity's out," Carina said. "Along with the engines, I think. Hsiao?"

"Yeah," the pilot replied grimly. "They took the brunt of the hit from the particle beam. We're dead in the water."

Only inertia was carrying the *Duchess* onward now.

"Particle beam?" asked Parthenia.

"From the *Peregrine*," Hsiao explained.

The other children were also coming around.

The pilot went on to briefly explain to them what had happened.

"I'll make some more elixir," Parthenia said, unfastening

the straps of her harness. She floated free, turned in the air, and gripped the back of her seat as if about to push herself toward the door.

"We don't have enough time," said Carina. She checked the interface. The destroyer had nearly caught up to them.

"We can still fight back," Ferne said. "We have weapons, and—"

"You're too young," interrupted Carina.

Then Atoi opened a comm to her. "We can't suit up. All the armor has been moved to the *Bathsheba,* so we'll just have to do without. When they get here, let me know where they're gonna come through."

"Shit," said Carina. She sagged, feeling utterly defeated. The *Peregrine* would catch them in minutes, and without power from the engines, the pulse cannons were dead. They'd fought so hard, and come so close to escape, but now the Regians were going to recapture them and take them to whatever horrors awaited on their planet. "The mages can't help you either. We're just about out of elixir. I hate to say it, but maybe we should surrender. If they take us to their planet, we might find a way—"

"What are you talking about?" Atoi's tone was harsh. "We *fight.* That's what the Black Dogs do—with or without armor and magical backup. If we die, it beats the alternative. Let me know where they're coming in."

The comm went dead.

At the same moment, the *Duchess* gave a slight judder.

The *Peregrine* had arrived.

But when Carina checked her interface, she saw the destroyer hadn't docked with the mercs' ship. Instead, a thick cable ran between the two vessels. The judder had been the impact of the grip on the end of the *Peregrine's* cable fastening onto the *Duchess's* hull.

As she watched, the cable tightened and straightened. The destroyer was beginning to slow down, and, now the vessels were joined, so would the mercs' ship.

"They aren't going to board us," she told the room.

"What?!" Hsiao exclaimed before also checking her screen. "Ugh. Cowards."

"The Regians are going to tow us back to the *Bathsheba*," Carina explained to her siblings, *Where*, she mentally added, *their huge numbers will overwhelm any defense we could mount.*

"Can we break the tow line?" Ferne asked.

"Without the engines, all our weapons are dead," replied Carina.

"Maybe we could Unlock it from the hull with a Cast?" Parthenia suggested. "We must have a little elixir left somewhere."

"They would just reattach it," said Carina. "Unless we have a Fix Destroyed Engines Cast, there's nothing we can do."

"Car," Atoi said angrily over her comm, "where—?"

"Nowhere, yet." She told her friend the situation.

Atoi's curse was cut off as she closed the comm.

The slowing of the *Duchess* increased abruptly, and Carina found herself thrown against her harness, hard. Parthenia flew across the bridge and hit the wall. She yelled with pain and remained spreadeagled against the vertical surface.

"Stay where you are," Carina called to her. "It's safer."

"I don't have a lot of choice about it," Parthenia replied.

After another minute, the bridge door opened. A hand grabbed each side of the doorway, and then Atoi glided in. She grabbed the back of Hsiao's seat to halt her progress.

"I have a suggestion," she said to Carina.

"I'd love to hear it."

Atoi glanced at the children, and pushed off from the pilot's seat to bring herself close to Carina. Holding onto an armrest while her legs floated in midair, she leaned down to bring her lips to Carina's ear. "The *Duchess* can self-destruct. Cadwallader told me about it when I got my promotion."

Carina reared back in shock. "*What the hell*? What happened to 'We fight'?"

"If it was just us against the Regians on the *Peregrine*, we might have stood a chance," Atoi replied quietly. "Not much of one, but a chance, nevertheless. If we go up against all the aliens aboard the *Bathsheba*, it'll be a massacre. Like I said, death beats the only alternative we have open to us right now."

Carina gazed at the faces of her brothers and sisters as they watched her and her friend, unsure of what was being discussed. They were so young, only beginning their lives. Was dying really the best the future had to offer them? She'd once thought so, after witnessing the suffering Ma had gone through —rape, imprisonment, slavery, torture. She'd risked so much for a chance at freedom for her family, thinking even if she died, even if they were all killed, it was better than living a life in torment.

Now, she was no longer so sure. So many times her family had been in situations that seemed hopeless, only for them to find a way out. No matter what they had to endure, there was always hope.

"We have to do it," Atoi urged. "At this distance we'll take out those fuckers on the destroyer, too."

Carina stared at her friend.

Risking death was one thing, but welcoming it with open arms?

"No," she said. "Absolutely not. I can't. I just can't."

Atoi's lips thinned to a line and her eyes narrowed. "Easy for you to say."

"What does *that* mean?"

"The Regians will keep *you* all alive," she spat. "The rest of us will be dishes on the menu."

She turned and propelled herself out of the room.

"Atoi!" Carina called after her. "Atoi!"

28

The mercs waited at the docking port. Though they weren't suited up, they'd found time during the short chase and retrieval of the *Duchess* to put on some clothes. A few were barefoot. Footwear hardly mattered in zero g. Perhaps they expected to die soon and never enter the artificial gravity of the *Bathsheba*.

Within the mercs' ship, Parthenia and Jace were guarding Darius and Nahla, and Ferne and Oriana were desperately trying to make elixir, but their attempts while the *Duchess* was being towed to the colony ship had all been failures. Sustaining a fire in zero g seemed impossible.

What does it matter? Carina thought. Even if the twins had managed to brew huge quantities of the stuff, the mages would only be able to forestall the inevitable. She couldn't see a way to defeat the hordes of Regians that awaited them, especially without armor to protect them from the creatures' deadly acid.

She could only hope that an opportunity to escape would open up.

Was Atoi right? Was she sacrificing the Black Dogs to a horrific fate in order to save the lives of her family?

The fact that her goal of returning to Earth had resulted in exposing her brothers and sisters to deathly danger many times weighed heavily enough on her mind as it was.

And then there was her execution of Sable Dirksen. If she hadn't killed the clan leader, the mercs might not even be there, Cadwallader might be alive...

She squeezed her eyes shut and pushed the thought away.

Thunk!

A jolt ended the forward progress of the *Duchess*. Most of the mercs were gripping handholds that lined the *Duchess's* walls, but a few glided forward and hit the docking port hatch in a jumble.

Jeers and insults erupted from the gathered soldiers as the unprepared men and women disentangled themselves to resume their positions, but Carina noticed an edge to the customary black-humored banter. The dark jokes about wanting to be appetizers for the Regians and going for chemical skin peels sounded hollow, even desperate.

Bryce was there, telling her with his eyes that he loved her. The young soldier who was Parthenia's friend was there too. Had the two of them had a chance to even speak?

Atoi's face was hard and determined. She was in fight mode, but Carina guessed her friend remained angry with her for refusing to agree to self-destruct the *Duchess*. What might her friend now suffer due to her decision?

She couldn't bear to think about it.

Tense seconds ticked past.

She strained her ears for the sound of the docking port being forced open, but no noises issued from it.

What were the Regians doing? Why weren't they trying to board the *Duchess* and recapture the failed escapees?

Atoi was cursing under her breath, and other mutterings arose among the rest of the mercs. Carina knew how they felt. The waiting was unbearable.

It was also deeply puzzling. What possible reason could the Regians have for the delay? Didn't they intend to enter the mercs' vessel at all? Did they plan on simply taking it along with the *Bathsheba* until they reached their planet?

A tiny flame of hope flared in her.

If the aliens were to leave them alone for a while—even a few hours—they could escape yet. The mages might figure out a way to make elixir, and she and Atoi would have time to think up a good plan.

Ideas began to race through her head. Perhaps they could rig up some kind of massive flamethrower. If they could take out hundreds of Regians at once, and if the mages could Split tens at a time, the mercs might be able to wipe up the rest.

"Hey, Atoi," Carina called.

But as her friend turned her head, the screech of a forced metal mechanism sounded from the docking port hatch, setting her teeth on edge.

The mercs readied their weapons.

"What?" said Atoi.

"Never mind."

The screech intensified and she winced at the painful noise.

"Ready..." Atoi warned.

Crack!

The hatch seal split, and the hatch swung inward. Beyond it lay the dimness of the Regian-infested *Bathsheba*. A puff of chilled atmosphere hit Carina's face. Figures moved in the darkness, but they were not the figures she'd expected to see.

"Fire!" yelled Atoi.

Pulses blazed from the mercs' rifles, turning twilight into day on the Regian side, revealing—not the aliens—but Mezban's soldiers. And toward the rear of them stood Mezban herself and Lomang.

The Regians had freed them and sent *them* to deal with the Black Dogs! The creatures had pitted human against human, relying on one side to betray the other. And it had worked. Mezban and Lomang had agreed to recapture the mercs and mages, perhaps in return for their own freedom.

Had it been the smuggler and his spouse who had come after them in the *Peregrine*? It would explain why it had taken so long before the *Duchess's* port had been forced open. They would have needed the time to dock their ship at the *Bathsheba*.

But the Regians' ploy might work in the Black Dogs' favor. The mercs were used to fighting other soldiers, and though their lack of armor was a big disadvantage, they might win.

Atoi was urging her soldiers forward, attempting to turn the defense into an offense. It was a desperate measure, but so was their situation. Also, they had a psychological edge. Mezban's troops would remember keenly that the mercs had defeated them once before and they might fear they would do so again. A forward push from the Black Dogs could trigger them into turning tail.

Carina berated herself for not spacing the lot of them, especially Mezban and Lomang. She hadn't spared the latter pair due to mercy, she'd simply been too busy arranging the mages and mercs' escape, and had assumed the Regians would take care of them.

The fighting intensified further as Mezban's soldiers fired volley after volley. The mercs were forced back and into the few available places to shelter.

Suddenly, something flew through the open port and landed with a metallic clunk.

"*Grenade!*" someone yelled.

A convulsion ran through the sheltering men and women.

A man ran forward, bent, and scooped up the device. Carina recognized him as Parthenia's friend. He made ready to throw the grenade back through the port, but before he could, he collapsed. He fell heavily, unconscious before he hit the floor, landing with the grenade underneath him.

The mercs closest to the man had begun to drop where they stood, their eyes closing and their knees buckling. The effect passed through the soldiers like an invisible ripple. A second after the first man had fallen, it hit her: the device one of Mezban's troops had thrown into the *Duchess* wasn't a grenade, it was a canister of gas—knockout gas. Within minutes it would be circulated through the air filtration system, and all aboard the *Duchess* would be unconscious and could be safely taken prisoner.

The gas reached her, and blackness swooped down.

29

Parthenia woke up lying on her back on what felt like cold, hard tile. She opened her eyes and found herself looking at a ceiling that seemed familiar, yet it was not at all what she expected to see.

Groggily, she tried to figure out what had happened. The last thing she could remember was being aboard the *Duchess*, trying to keep Darius and Nahla occupied while the Regians towed the ship to the *Bathsheba*. Nahla had been telling a fanciful story about a kingdom of horses, the animals they'd ridden on Pirine. The animals could talk and they were debating about which of them should be their new king and queen. Darius had been watching her, entranced as always when she wove her tales.

She'd felt the ship had come to a halt, which meant they'd reached their destination, and she'd been thinking that if the Black Dogs failed to fight off the Regians—an almost impossible task—the aliens would soon come for her and her siblings.

Oriana and Ferne had been struggling to start a fire. If only they had more elixir! The twins had enclosed splinters of wood in a wire mesh to hold them together in the zero g, and...

Where was she?

She shook the fog from her mind. As she sat up she recognized her surroundings immediately. She was in the *Bathsheba's* refectory, where Lomang and Mezban had imprisoned the mercs after taking them out of stasis. And they were all back here again: around her lay, sat, and stood the men and women of the Black Dogs.

She started in fear. Where were her brothers and sisters? She swung around, and then exhaled in relief. All her siblings except Carina were lying behind her, still unconscious.

What had happened, and where was her sister? How had she and everyone else gotten from the mercs' ship to the colony vessel? She couldn't recall a thing since that final moment in the *Duchess's* galley.

"Hey!"

Parthenia looked up and saw Carina standing over her. Her sister reached out a hand and pulled her to her feet.

They hugged, and Carina looked her in the eyes. "How are you feeling?"

"Okay. I just don't understand—"

"They gassed the ship. Knocked us all unconscious. Then they carried us here, I guess. Are you sure you're okay?"

"Yes, just about," Parthenia replied, though in truth she still felt befuddled.

"Good. Do you still have your translator and comm?"

She put a hand to her chest and touched her ear. "I do. I never took them off."

"Great. I have mine, too. It'll help a lot if we can understand what the Regians are saying."

"I suppose it will. I..." She rubbed her forehead. "Sorry, I'm still groggy."

On the floor next to her, Ferne and Oriana were beginning

to stir, though Darius and Nahla remained out of it, perhaps because their smaller bodies took longer to process the gas.

Carina said, "I know it's a lot to handle. Parthenia, you were a tremendous help to me before, when we set the bomb and escaped. If it weren't for Lomang and Mezban, we might have made it. Now we're gonna have to pull another stunt or two. Are you up to it? I need you."

"Of course. Of course I'll help."

Carina squeezed her upper arm then she strode off, no doubt on her way to talk to someone about a plan she had.

Parthenia was gratified and comforted by her sister's praise and faith in her. It seemed their relationship had turned a corner. The change in Carina's attitude had been a long time coming, but now it had arrived it was very welcome.

She spotted Jace, who was talking to Bryce. She waved to get the mage's attention, hoping he would come over to her. She wanted to talk to him but she didn't want to leave the children alone. They would be confused and scared as they came around.

Jace noticed her, said something to Bryce, and began to head toward her when the refectory doors suddenly drew back. Armed soldiers poured in, barking orders, telling everyone to move back.

The mercs froze for a moment, hesitating. Then a group—Atoi among them—rushed the troops, trying to grab their weapons, but the soldiers quickly responded with stun rounds and cracked their rifle butts on the resisters' skulls. The skirmish was soon over, and the remaining Black Dogs waited, tense and angry.

Meanwhile, the rest of Mezban's troops formed a wedge, its point protruding into the room and the wide base blocking the exit. The soldiers at the outer edge of the formation scanned the prisoners until one pointed at something and spoke to his buddy. The two marched forward, joined by a third.

They were heading for Carina.

Mercs drew together in front of her, but the soldiers aimed their rifles at them. Carina pushed her defenders aside and walked from between them to meet the oncoming soldiers.

One of them took out a black bag as another went behind her and tied her wrists together.

Carina's gaze sought Parthenia's. Just before the bag was lowered over her head, she called out, "Look after the kids!"

"I will!" Parthenia shouted back, her heart in her mouth.

She watched, aghast, as the soldiers led Carina away, guiding her roughly by pushing her back. She stumbled, and a soldier dragged her to her feet, drawing rumbles of displeasure from the Black Dogs.

She disappeared into the wedge of soldiers, and a line of disturbance formed as she was led through them and out of the room.

"Parthenia, where are we?" Darius asked.

He'd finally woken up, and so had Nahla. Oriana and Ferne were now fully conscious, but they'd remained quiet, apparently immediately understanding the gravity of the situation.

"Shh," Parthenia whispered to Darius. "Don't move. Stay down."

As she returned her attention to Mezban's troops, another of them lifted an arm and pointed.

He was pointing at her!

She started and took a step back.

Again, three soldiers marched out from the wedge.

"NO!" a voice in the crowd yelled.

She saw Kamil running toward her, but a soldier fired at him. He fell, hitting his head on the edge of a table as he went down.

"Kamil!" Parthenia called out. She managed only a few steps in his direction before the soldiers had reached her. One grabbed her arm and twisted it behind her back. She screamed in pain.

"Don't hurt my sister!" Darius yelled.

"Let me go!" Parthenia pleaded. She couldn't be taken away like Carina. She had to stay with her brothers and sisters.

She struggled and fought, but the men were much stronger than she was. Her other arm was pulled inexorably behind her, large, rough hands drew her wrists together, and something snapped closed around them.

With horror, she saw a black bag open in front of her face.

She fought again, desperately trying to wrench herself free, dreading the idea of the suffocating black material over her head.

She heard Nahla cry out, "Leave her alone!"

"No, please!" she begged. "Please! I have to stay with—"

The bag descended and darkness smothered her.

Again, she screamed. She writhed and kicked, threshing like a wild thing.

Pain exploded in her stomach. She'd been stunned.

She had a faint sensation of hands lifting her, but after that, nothing.

30

T he next time Parthenia woke up she was in utter darkness and the air felt unbearably humid and close. She could barely breathe. When she tried to move, her wrists sent out stabbing pains and her arms ached.

She turned her head, and her mouth touched textile. Instantly, everything came flooding back: Mezban's soldiers, Carina being taken away, the black bag over her head, and the stunning pulse round.

She twisted and felt a flat, smooth surface underneath her. Her wrists complained louder. Panic rose in her. She couldn't bear the idea of the bag covering her eyes, nose, and mouth. Her breathing quickened until she was panting—panting in fear. What if the bag didn't allow in enough air? She already felt light-headed and nauseated.

Am I already running out of oxygen?

"Help!" she called. "Please, take this bag off me. Please!"

The thick material muffled her voice.

She struggled to sit up, wriggling her shoulders and pressing down with her sore wrists. Sweat prickled her face and neck. When she was finally sitting, she leaned forward and shook her head, trying to dislodge the stifling bag.

Then she had an idea. She bent farther forward and opened her knees. As soon as she felt the material of the bag brush her kneecaps, she closed her knees again. Holding them together firmly, she lifted her head, drawing off the bag.

She was still in darkness, but now she could breathe. As she leaned back in relief, her back hit a wall. She reached out with her fingertips to touch it: cold metal. She shuffled sideways on her bottom and quickly encountered another wall. Moving in the opposite direction brought the same result.

Parthenia tried to stand, but before she rose much higher than a kneeling position, the crown of her head struck the ceiling. She walked forward on her knees. A few 'steps' brought her to a fourth wall.

She appeared to be inside a windowless metal box, every dimension measuring less than a meter and a half. The panic she'd successfully fought off began to return.

Her pulse raced. How long would she have to stay there? Would the Regians leave her there forever?

No. They wanted her mage skills. It made no sense to let her suffocate or die of thirst.

Yet she couldn't rid herself of the fear. She lay down and curled up on her side, closing her eyes against the darkness. Images of her brothers and sisters as she'd last seen them in the *Bathsheba's* refectory flickered through her mind. Where were they all now? Were they all inside metal cubes like her? Were they alone and frightened too? Tears dripped from the side of her face onto the floor.

So much for her brave assertion that she would help Carina. All the Regians had to do was put her in a box and she was a wreck.

Through her feelings of weakness and helplessness, she

became aware of a vibration through the floor and realized she recognized the sensation—it was the throb of a starship engine.

Was she still aboard the *Bathsheba*? She didn't recall noticing the vibration of the colony ship's engines before. She'd assumed the vessel's size dampened them out. So, if she wasn't on the *Bathsheba*, was she on the Regians' ship? Or was she already aboard a shuttlecraft and being taken down to their planet?

Their world had to be her final destination. What would happen there? She shuddered. The aliens would want her to Cast for them, that much was certain. Should she? Or should she fake terror like she had before? Not very much faking would be required.

PARTHENIA DIDN'T KNOW how long she'd been trapped inside the cube except that it seemed like hours. She'd pushed against all the sides, the ceiling, and the floor until she was exhausted. After that, she'd lain on her side for a long time, trying to mentally still her fears.

Finally, she'd fallen asleep and dreamt about being trapped at the bottom of a deep well, the water inside gradually rising. She could see the bright circle of the opening, and peering down at her was her father, laughing and waving. She called out to him as the water rose above her shoulders and crept up her neck, imploring him to throw down a rope and pull her up, but he'd only laughed louder.

When the water was above her nose, she woke up, at first relieved to realize she'd only been having a nightmare, and then despairing when she understood she remained in the metal box.

With some difficulty, she turned over in order to ease her aching body. She felt like crying again, but she was all out of tears. In all the dangerous and terrifying situations she'd been in since Carina had rescued her and her siblings from the Sherrerrs' ship, *Nightfall*, she didn't think she'd encountered any quite as horrible or dire as this.

As she lay down on her other side, however, she noticed something had changed. Something was different. She sat up and looked around, trying to penetrate the pitch dark that surrounded her. No chink of light offered itself, and no breath of current stirred the air, yet she was certain she wasn't imagining the alteration.

She inhaled sharply. The floor was no longer vibrating.

Before she had time to process the fact, one side of the box suddenly fell open and hit the floor with a deafening clang.

Parthenia grimaced as light and chill air flooded in. She blinked and shivered, catching a glimpse of the interior of a chamber and, through an opening, a dark gray landscape beyond.

A Regian stepped in front of her, obscuring her view with its long, articulated legs.

She uttered a short scream and drew back.

The lid of the box lifted and the remaining sides collapsed. More Regians stood around her. She cringed, drawing in her shoulders and knees.

No eyes. No see. No eyes. No see.

The voices were coming from her comm. She still had the translator hanging around her neck.

No eyes, no see? What did the Regians mean? Were they going to put out her eyes?

Sheer terror overcame her. She leapt to her feet on wobbling legs and tried to run.

A pincered leg rose and pushed her shoulder, hard, and she toppled down, but not as hard as she expected. She realized she felt curiously light. The gravity on the Regians' planet was less than standard.

Two more sets of pincers picked up the black bag lying on the floor of the box.

"No," Parthenia said, "not that. Not that again! I'll keep my eyes closed, I promise."

But if the Regians understood her, they didn't care about her horror of the bag. In another moment it was over her head again.

Pincers plucked at her clothes and then fastened on her shirt with a firm hold before dragging her upward. The curved tips of more pincers prodded her back and backside, encouraging her to move.

She managed to stagger upright and walk in the direction the Regians pushed her.

Walking in darkness knowing she couldn't break her fall with her hands if she tripped was deeply unnerving. Where were they taking her and what would happen when she arrived? Did they understand that she needed elixir in order to Cast? How would she communicate the ingredients she needed or the process? And if she couldn't make them understand, what would they do? She'd heard the Regians regarded humans as food. If they thought she was useless to them, would they...?

She swallowed and concentrated on putting one foot in front of the other. Almost as bad as her horror of being eaten alive was her concern for her brothers and sisters. Protecting her siblings had been part of her life for as far back as she could remember, first from their father and later from the many dangers that had faced them. But now they were beyond her care. Would she ever see them again?

She decided she would do whatever she could to survive. She would Cast for the aliens. They weren't like her father. They didn't understand the things mages could do. She would find out where Carina and her other siblings were being held, and they would escape the Regians' world together, somehow.

Then she remembered Kamil. Was he already on the planet too? She needed to find him and the rest of the mercenaries. She couldn't leave them all there to be eaten.

The stony ground she'd been walking across suddenly sloped downward, and she stumbled. Her knees impacted sharp edges that cut into her skin. She cried out in pain as Regian words came through her comm: *Move. Walk. Step. Walk. Run.*

She climbed to her feet, her breath puffing out the material of the bag, and felt blood dribble down her legs. She walked on carefully, trying to avoid falling again onto the ridged ground. The slope grew steeper until she was struggling to remain upright, though the ridges helped her to grip the ground.

As she'd been walking, a rustling noise had risen around her—a noise that was horribly familiar. She knew from the fight with the Regians in the *Bathsheba's* gym that she was hearing the creatures' bodies rub up against each other. She was clearly in some kind of Regian habitation.

After she'd been walking for about twenty minutes, the ground quickly evened out and she could tread more easily again.

A jab from a pincer to her right pushed her in another direction. A new, gentler slope appeared beneath her feet, and at the same time an odor arose from the base of the bag enclosing her head: a musty, cloying, sickening stench, like the local fungus her father used to like to eat on Ithiya mixed with the smell of rotting meat.

Something long and hard cracked against her shins and she tumbled forward, her face smacking into the ground. But it didn't hurt badly. The low, sharp ridges had been replaced by a soft substance that cushioned her fall.

Before she could rise again, the bag was ripped from her head.

31

"I told you once I was your nemesis," said Mezban, smirking, "and I was correct."

Carina knelt at the woman's feet, held there by Pappu's hand on her shoulder. She guessed the audience with Mezban and Lomang was a short stop on her way to somewhere else, in the company of the Regians.

The aliens crowded at the door of the small room where Mezban and Lomang sat. She could hear the creatures' words through her comm: *Bring them. Soon. Enough. Near. Finish.*

"This isn't over yet," Carina replied. "You're going to regret what you've done, and then we'll see who's the nemesis around here."

"You're right," said Mezban. "It isn't over. Though for you it will be shortly. But before you go to live out the rest of your sad life incarcerated on the Regians' planet, I want something. Tell me where you've hidden the ember gems. I know you must have taken them from the *Zenobia*."

Mezban leaned forward and her dark hair hung down, partially obscuring her face, but her eyes glinted like the precious stones of which she spoke.

Carina had almost forgotten about the jewelry Lomang had stolen from his wife, prompting her to follow his sorry ass all the way to another galactic sector. She'd only given a couple of the beautiful gems as payment for repairing and refitting the *Duchess* and upgrading the Black Dogs' armor and equipment.

It took her a moment to recall what had happened to the rest, then she remembered: at the beginning of their journey, after the mercs had captured the *Bathsheba*, she'd put the stones in a safe in a storage room, along with the ancient mage documents.

"I don't have the jewels anymore," she replied. "I traded them all at Martha's Rest."

Mezban snorted with laughter. "For *what*? A city? A country? That's their worth."

"How was I to know their value?" Carina asked. "I got what I needed with them. That was all I cared about."

The likelihood of her ever seeing the stones again was looking extremely remote, but she was damned if she was going to give them up to this despicable traitor of her own kind.

"So it was you who came after us in the destroyer?" she continued. "I thought it was the Regians."

"It was indeed," Lomang replied, his hands folded on his fattened belly. "We offered, you see, knowing only the *Peregrine* could catch you and incapacitate your ship."

"You're even stupider than I thought," Carina said. "You did the Regians' dirty work when you could have flown away freely."

"That would have meant giving up the ember gems," replied Mezban.

"But you would have gotten away with your lives. Do you really think the Regians are going to just let you leave?"

"They will." Lomang nodded sagely, repeating, "They will. But you won't see it. After you and your family are gone, we will return to our home world and live out our lives in peace. And perhaps one day we will have the opportunity to purchase another inter-sector ship, and we will journey again into your sector and relieve it of the best of its wares." He winked at her.

"Not without my jewels, we won't!" Mezban spat, giving her husband a deathly glare.

He ducked his head, immediately subdued.

Mezban rose to her feet. "Where are they?!"

Carina smiled. "I told you. I don't have any left. And even if I did have some hidden away somewhere, what are you going to threaten me with if I refuse to hand them over? Imprisonment? Torture? My family turned into slaves? The Black Dogs consumed by monsters?"

The woman strode over and slapped her hard across her cheek.

"Is that the best you've got?" Carina asked, unfazed. "I'd leave the beating of the prisoners to your brother-in-law if I were you."

"Tell me where you've hidden my gems!" Mezban stamped one of her little feet. "Or Pappu will batter you within an inch of your life."

Carina shrugged. "It wouldn't be for the first time, and he won't actually kill me. You can't afford to anger the Regians."

Nai Nai had taught her mind control techniques that would enable her to shut out the pain from a sustained beating, though she would feel the effects as she recovered. She was more worried about her siblings, as well as Bryce, Jace, and the Black Dogs. She was the only one who knew the location of the gems. If Mezban got it into her tiny mind that someone else might also be privy to the secret, she might attempt to extract it from them by force.

Voices came through her comm: *Finish. No wait. Bring them. Soon.*

"So you've lost the *Bathsheba*, all the contraband you were smuggling, and the ember gems, and now you're about to lose your miserable lives," said Carina. "It might not look like it just yet, but I think I'm actually going to come out the winner here. My family and I will survive, and soon we'll have our liberty too. The Regians might keep us captive for a short while but we'll find a way to escape. It isn't hard for mages."

"We will *not* lose our lives!" Mezban seethed. "It is *you* who has lost. You've lost everything!"

Carina looked over her shoulder at the Regians who were gathered in the doorway. "You know what? Regians have been raiding the district where I grew up for hundreds of years, so long, in fact, they've become part of the local mythology. The same is true in your culture, right? That means they've been capturing humans and bringing them here for a very long time, easily long enough to learn our languages well. I bet they understand more of our speech than you think.

"My guess is they've overheard both of you talking about the ember gems, and the only reason they're allowing us this time together is because they want to discover the stones' location for themselves. If I were to tell you where I *may* have hidden them, they'll have everything they wanted: mages, the Black Dogs, you and your soldiers, and, finally, the ember gems. As soon as I name the hiding place, they'll probably come in here right away to grab you."

Mezban's features fell, and she glanced at her husband.

He returned her gaze with fear in his eyes.

"You *have* discussed the jewels around the Regians, haven't you?" asked Carina.

Pallor overtaking the rich olive of her skin, Mezban returned uncertainly to her seat.

"It's all nonsense," said Pappu, his deep voice rumbling. "Your soldiers are armed, Mezban. The Regians would never have allowed them to carry weapons if they didn't intend to let us leave."

Lomang relaxed and grinned. "You're right, dear brother."

He turned to his wife. "Pappu speaks the truth, my dear. We have nothing to fear. The mage is only trying to beguile us, as is her way. We mustn't listen to her drivel." He focused on Carina. "You have one chance remaining to tell us where you hid the gems, or suffer the consequences." Leaning forward and narrowing his eyes, he said, "You *can* do your magic with only one hand, right?"

"Are you *sure* your soldiers are still armed?" she asked. "Do you even know where they are?"

Mezban started with alarm and peered beyond the Regians outside the room.

"Take no notice," Lomang said. "She's only trying to frighten and confuse us. I'm warning you, one final chance," he said to Carina.

She sighed. "I guess there's only one way of finding out which of us is right."

"No," Mezban blurted. "No, we no longer want to know where the jewels are. Lomang, we must leave now."

"I'm telling you she's fooling us, dear wife. She's only angry she must give up the gems to us before she enters into slavery. She hopes to get her revenge by tricking us into leaving without them."

"I do not want the stones!" Mezban exclaimed.

"You don't?" Carina asked. "Oh, but I insist. Let me tell you where you can find them. They're—"

"Be silent!" yelled Mezban. "Pappu, knock her out. I don't want her to utter another word. Lomang, if you don't come with me, I'm leaving without you. I'll take the *Peregrine,* and the Regians can have you."

"Pappu, don't touch her," said Lomang. "Let her speak."

Pappu looked from the wife to the husband, as if unsure who to obey.

"You idiot!" Mezban shrieked at Lomang. "You cretin! Why did I ever marry you? You've brought me nothing but trouble.

You're too stupid even to understand how stupid you are! You've stolen from me, lied, cheated, dragged me into your ridiculous schemes, and ruined my life!"

The small woman was working herself into a paroxysm of fury. Her face glowed red, her eyes looked about to pop from their sockets, and her hands clenched and unclenched at her sides.

Despite her personal worries, Carina couldn't help but chuckle. Lomang was dumb, sure enough, but so was Mezban, just in a different way. If the woman had been smart, she would have left a couple of minutes ago and been on her way to her ship. The Regians might have been caught unawares, and she could have escaped if she knew how to fly a starship.

But, instead, her temper had gotten the better of her. She'd missed her opportunity, and now she was going to pay.

Carina stood up. "I hid the gems in the viewing dome," she said quietly.

None of the humans present heard her. Lomang was attempting to soothe his irate wife while she ranted and railed at him, hitting his chest with her little fists, and Pappu was watching them with sad resignation.

Carina cleared her throat and repeated herself, louder. "I hid the gems in the viewing dome."

Mezban heard her and turned, her jaw dropping open, words drying in her mouth.

The Regians shifted restlessly, scraping their carapaces against each other.

Carina faced the aliens. "The viewing dome, at the top of the ship, where I set the bomb. I hid the gems behind the bar. They might still be there."

Though Lomang and Mezban were out of sight behind her, she was sure she could *feel* them freeze.

The aliens stopped moving, and for a moment all was silent and still.

Then hell broke loose.

Regians surged into the room and grabbed Carina with their pincers, tugging her toward the door. She looked back.

Mezban screamed as the aliens reached her. Pappu tried to run and was drowned in a sea of black carapaces. Lomang gaped when the creatures descended on him, appearing amazed at this ill turn of fate against all his expectations.

As Carina was dragged away and the black bag was thrust over her head once more, she smiled a grim smile of satisfaction.

32

Parthenia vigorously rubbed the two pieces of organic, fibrous material together again. She'd lost count of the times she'd performed the same action, all with the identical result: no fire. Not even a thread of smoke. Her fingers were raw from her efforts, and her back ached from crouching over the shallow depression she'd dug in the floor of the pit where the Regians had put her.

The method had worked for Ferne on Ostillon when Carina had Transported them to different places on the planet, and she was sure she was doing it right according to what he'd told her. Perhaps the material was too damp.

Everything was damp down there in the Regian city. The air was so humid it was as if you could wring water out of it. Her hair had turned into a ball of frizz and her clothes felt moist to the touch. It was also cold. She was chilled to the bone, and she could almost feel the water in the atmosphere leaching the heat from her.

If only she could make a fire. It wouldn't only allow her to Cast as the Regian king had commanded, the flames would also help to keep her warm. She was no splicer, but she knew her health would quickly decline in the conditions and she might only have days to live.

A shadow moved above her, shifting the meager light that penetrated her pit from the Regian metropolis above.

Her guard was checking on her again.

Ready. Now. King.

"No," she replied. "I'm not ready. I can't make fire. Can you bring me some type of fire? I need naked flames. If you can do that I'll Cast for your king."

Not word. Ready. Now. King.

"No!" she exclaimed, standing up. "I need fire! Fire, fire, fire! Why can't you understand? How can you not know what fire is? One of the first things humans learned to do was to make fire, hundreds of thousands of years ago, when we were hardly more than animals. How can you build cities and starships and yet you can't make fire?"

Not word. King wait. Anger. Ready. Infest family.

"Ugh." She shuddered. She didn't know exactly what the guard meant by 'infest family' but it sounded bad, whatever it was. "Please apologize to your king for me. Say I'm really sorry, I need more time."

The guard didn't move for some moments, then the light shifted again and the creature was gone.

Parthenia flopped down and picked up the pieces of fibrous material again. Doggedly, she rubbed them together over the shredded fibers in the depression. The guard had tried to bring her everything she'd asked for. The container seemed to be fashioned from a shell and the opening was a little too narrow, but it would suffice; the water was so murky she hadn't dared to drink it yet, though she was dreadfully thirsty, the metal—how did the Regians have metal if they couldn't understand the concept of fire?—the metal was perfect: fine filings.

Perhaps the only problem was that the aliens didn't know

the word 'fire'. They definitely appeared to struggle to understand her in other things she'd said to them.

She stopped rubbing and held up the objects in her hands for inspection. Each about the size of her fist, they were flat on one side and tangled with something like bristles on the other. The inner surfaces had worn smooth from friction. At first, she'd thought they might be a kind of root from a tree or shrub, but now she wasn't at all confident the material was wood.

Recalling her glimpse of the landscape she'd seen before, she wouldn't have been surprised if no trees grew on the Regian planet. She hadn't seen any vegetation, and the sky had been thick with dark clouds. Perhaps she'd arrived there in the evening but she had a feeling the place was always like that. On the *Bathsheba,* the aliens had set the lights to low levels, which must have been how they felt most comfortable.

If their world didn't contain any wood then her efforts were hopeless. She would never make elixir, never Cast for the king, and her family would be 'infested', whatever that meant. She would probably be infested too.

Parthenia put down the pieces of material she was holding and wrapped her arms around herself, trying to retain the remaining warmth in her body. She sniffed as thin mucus threatened to drip from her nose.

If she couldn't Cast, perhaps there was another answer to her predicament.

She mentally went over what she knew.

When the bag had been taken off her head, the first sight to greet her was a bloated creature that looked nothing like the other Regians. Its thick, segmented body lay directly on the floor of the chamber, about two meters wide and tall and an unknown length as she'd been unable to see the end of it. If the creature had legs, they were clearly not substantial enough to bear its weight.

At one of his sides, Regians were collecting small, egg-shaped objects the alien seemed to be producing from some-where in its large bulk.

The chamber had been as dark as everywhere else, lit only by phosphorescent spots on the ceiling. The walls were sleek and dark, while the floor was soft and damp, like thick, deep, leaf mold in an old forest.

She'd been too terrified to speak at first, but as the silence surrounding her grew, she understood that the aliens expected her to say something.

What should she say? If she said the wrong thing she might immediately be hauled off to a Regian kitchen.

Bizarrely, the lessons in diplomacy and oratory she'd taken while growing up on Ithiya came to the forefront of her mind. She stood up slowly, watching for signs from the Regians surrounding her that her behavior was acceptable. When she was upright, she bowed.

"My name is Parthenia."

Alien. Host. Special. Alien. Creature. King. Perform. Illusion. Special. Creature. Power.

She touched her ear comm. The deluge of words was over-whelming. "Please, just one of you speak. I can't understand you."

King. I king. Alien.

King? The creature looked the least like any king she could have imagined.

She assumed the 'alien' was her. She bowed again. "I am very pleased to meet you, king."

Special illusion. Creature. Power.

"It is not an illusion, er...your Majesty. I do have a special power, which I would be happy to offer in your service."

Serving the king of the Regians was the last thing she wanted to do, but some dissembling could buy her the time and oppor-tunity she needed to rescue the people the aliens had captured.

Power. Show. Ability. Perform. Alien.

"I can't do it without elixir. If you will allow me to make the liquid I need, I will demonstrate my power."

Liquid. Bring. Power.

"Yes, the liquid helps to give me my power."

Bring. Liquid. Ability.

A moment later something poked her back. A Regian was standing behind her carrying a bowl filled with an opaque fluid that might have been water.

"No, not water," she said to the king. "I need elixir. Only *I* can make it, if you can give me..."

She'd told the creature everything she needed, but it appeared her requests would take some time to fulfill, because the Regians had removed her from her audience with the king and taken her to the pit.

Along the way, she'd seen parts of the habitation. The aliens lived underground, which wasn't surprising considering the barren hostility of life on the surface. The tough, chitinous substance that comprised the walls and ceiling in the king's chamber was the material of choice for the low, windowless rooms that lined the passages. The creatures also seemed to favor the soft, dank floors everywhere she passed. Perhaps it was comfortable for their pincered feet.

The end to her journey, when it had come, had been abrupt and unexpected. One moment she'd been walking down a dimly lit thoroughfare, flanked by two Regians on each side, and the next, one of them had sharply shoved her and she'd found herself falling down a near-vertical slope.

In the poor light conditions she hadn't noticed the hole in the ground she'd been pushed into. She had a split second to fear the impact at the bottom before she hit it, though the soft landing and low gravity meant she was unhurt. After a few moments, her eyes adjusted to the even lower level of light, and she'd seen she was basically in a hole in the ground, about three meters wide.

There was nothing for her to sit or lie on, no food and no water. The opening to the shaft she'd fallen down was beyond her reach, though the shaft itself was only a couple of meters long.

Summing up her situation, it didn't look good. She wasn't ever going to be able to make elixir. Eventually, the king's patience would run out, and her family would be 'infested'.

She had to try something else, and she had to act fast.

33

Atoi's words were echoing in Carina's head: *Easy for you to say. The Regians will keep you all alive. The rest of us will be dishes on the menu.*

Her friend was right, of course.

The powers she'd often considered as much of a disadvantage as a benefit, the ability that made mages a target for exploitation, could be the very thing to save her and her family. But the realization brought her little joy. The men and women of the Black Dogs had always been more than hired mercenaries to her. She'd grown from a kid to a woman among them, and, though they'd first fought for her because they were being paid, the lines of her relationship with them had softened since then. They'd joined her on the epic journey across the galaxy. They were no longer employees but companions.

She couldn't allow them to come to harm on the Regians' planet. When she figured out a way to escape, she wouldn't be leaving unless she could bring every single merc with her.

She'd slumped against the side of the box that the aliens had confined her in. It was the most comfortable position she could find in the small cube. From the movements she'd felt, she guessed she'd arrived on the aliens' world, and it was only a matter of time until—

One side of the box fell open, and a cold, damp, gust of air blew in. Carina shivered and peered out into darkness. She'd expected to see something brighter than the pitch black of the box's interior, but if it hadn't been for the sound of the side falling and the fresh breeze, she wouldn't have known what had happened. She guessed it was nighttime and cloudy. Her body felt light, and she recalled the planet's low gravity.

The lid of the box lifted and the remaining sides collapsed.

She shivered. The chill wind was almost a gale, and she couldn't see a thing.

She could hear stuff, though: the familiar rustle of Regians' carapaces in contact with each other.

Pincers plucked at her clothes, encouraging her to rise.

"You can talk to me," she said. "I can understand you."

Neither Lomang nor Mezban had thought to take the translator from her, either due to their stupidity or because they didn't think they would need it. She guessed they were regretting the omission now. Or maybe not. Maybe it was better to not hear how your captors planned to fricassee you.

No eyes. No see. No eyes. No see.

"Dammit. You want me to wear the stupid bag? Go ahead. Put it back on me. I'm as good as blind right now anyway."

Removing the bag had been the first thing she'd done after the creatures had forced her into the box. The Regians clearly didn't want her to see their ship or wherever they planned to take her now.

The small sack was thrust over her head, and the aliens began to prod her back.

"*Okay.* I'm moving, see?"

She shuffled forward, feeling with her toes for unevenness

and obstacles. At the same time, she strained her ears, listening for sounds of the Regians' other captives—her family, in particular. The kids would be terrified, though Parthenia would be able to provide some comfort and help to keep them safe.

What would she do without her sister? She hoped she'd finally healed the rift between them.

Suddenly, the ground disappeared from beneath her feet and she plummeted.

She screamed, but her cry was cut off as she hit a soft surface, falling quickly to her knees and then onto her side.

Pincers poked her body. She heard a snip, and her hands were free.

Instantly, she ripped the bag from her head, just in time to see the door to her new confinement close.

Here, there was light, and odor—a terrible odor.

She jumped up and ran to the grid that separated her from her surroundings. The Regian who had cut through the binding around her wrists and closed her cage door was leaving.

She could see no other aliens in the place, only humans.

Clutching the wires in horror and dismay, Carina's gaze roved over the scene, her mind almost unable to take in what she was seeing.

Hundreds of people lay on the ground, under a strange pale green light emitted by some kind of phosphorescent plant on the ceiling. The people were unclothed and lying face upward, alive but barely moving. The reason for their position was obvious: each person had a pillow-shaped object fixed to their stomach. Strings of these hard, oblong cases hung from the ceiling to the floor.

The sight sparked a flashback. She'd seen the strings before, in the *Bathsheba's* viewing dome, when she and Parthenia had gone there to plant the bomb.

What were they? Why had the Regians stuck them to the people's stomachs?

She reached through the metal grid. "Hey!" she called to the nearest person, who lay only a few meters away. "Hey! Can you hear me?"

The woman's eyes flickered and her mouth moved but no sounds came out.

Then Carina saw the source of the sickening stench. Only the people nearest to her were alive. Beyond them, in the center of the underground space, lay corpses. Blackened and rotting, some almost skeletal, they also carried the Regians' cases on their stomachs, though these cases had softened and collapsed.

She dropped to her knees, and tears of dismay and pity filled her eyes. *This* was what happened to the people the Regians took from the poor settlements they raided. To be eaten would at least be a quick death, not this dreadful torture.

In happier times, as a child, she'd loved to study insects. She'd found everything about them fascinating: what they ate, the homes they built for themselves, how they reproduced, and their life cycles. An idea of what was happening to the people before her forced its way into her stricken mind, and she turned to one side and vomited.

A scream cut through the torment of her thoughts.

The sound abruptly stopped, and she heard a dull, soft *thump.*

Someone else had fallen into the chamber.

She heard a child weeping.

"Who's that?" she called out. "Is that you, Darius? Nahla?"

The sobs stopped. "Carina?" Oriana replied. "You're here too? Ugh, what's that awful smell?"

It was difficult to see in the dim light, but from the direction of her voice Oriana appeared to have been dropped into a cell on the other side of the chamber.

"Yes. I'm opposite you, I think," she said. "Oriana, do you have a bag over your head? If you do, don't take it off."

What could she tell her sister to explain why? She had to prevent her from seeing the heart-wrenching, dreadful spectacle of the Regians' other human captives.

"Huh?"

"Just don't take the bag off!"

"Uh, uh..." Oriana began to hyperventilate. Carina could hear her great whoops of breath across the chamber.

"It's horrible, horrible!" she said after a minute, when she seemed to get over her shock a little. "Carina, what's happening to those poor people?"

"I don't know," she replied, though she thought she did. "Try not to look at them. I don't think there's anything we can do to help them."

Ferne arrived next, and Carina went through the same process with her brother.

When Darius and Nahla were dropped into the chamber, she thought she might have better success at persuading them to leave their bags on but she didn't. The youngest children also saw the horror.

As far as she could tell, her brothers and sisters were confined at roughly equal distances apart around the circular space. To her right and left stood cells like hers, empty but with the doors in the metal grid walls open. The Regians seemed to want to keep the mages as far apart as they could.

Nahla was the last to arrive. After Carina had done her best to calm her little sister, she waited for the expected fifth sibling, but she didn't arrive.

Finally, she asked, "When was the last time you saw Parthenia?"

Oriana replied, "We haven't seen her for a long time. The soldiers took her right after they took you."

"You don't know what happened to her?"

"No," said Ferne. "We all came here together, but not Parthenia. We don't know where she is."

"What?!"

Shit.

Where was the oldest of her sisters?

34

Parthenia's heart drummed against her breastbone as she contemplated what she was about to do. Time was running out fast. The guard could come back any minute, and if she was caught the Regians would put her somewhere from which she had zero prospect of escape.

She had to *move*.

But her limbs seemed frozen.

Hot blood generated by fear had driven out the intense chill that had invaded her body, and her skin was slick with sweat.

"I'm going to do it," she murmured. "I *will* do it."

Still, she remained motionless.

"Now. I'm doing it now!"

Somehow, she forced her reluctant arm to reach out. She dug her fingers into the wall and pulled out a large chunk. Like the floor, the material felt very soft and damp.

She dropped the chunk and pulled out another handful with her other hand.

Casting the stuff aside, she grabbed the edges of the hole she'd made and pulled them away, widening the gap. It had to be at least as wide as her.

What would come next made her gasp with trepidation, but now that she'd begun, she knew she wouldn't stop. Not unless she died in her attempt.

She ripped into the wall, yanking out thick pieces and creating a pile on the floor. When the hole was deep and wide enough, she would be able to stand on the pile to climb into the hole. From then on, she only had to dig, dig upward, all the way to the surface, dropping the humus below her.

Within a minute, she'd made a deep hole and she was struggling to reach the top of it to pull out more material. She tried standing on the pile, but it squashed down nearly flat under her weight.

Darn it!

Parthenia jumped to reach further and succeeded in deepening the hole, but soon she was stymied again.

It wasn't going to work, not this way.

She took a break, panting, as she tried to figure out a solution.

Above her, the steady, dull light dimmed.

She held her breath. Had the guard come back?

But the light returned to its usual subdued level. It had only been something passing above—another Regian.

What would she do if she was spotted after she escaped?

Parthenia shook her head. She would have to work that out later.

The tunnel she was digging was too perpendicular, she realized. She had to make it run at more of an angle. It meant more digging, which would take more time, but she had no choice.

Thrusting her already sore hands into the wall, she began to tear at its lower surface, creating a deeper slope. As soon as there was sufficient room, she climbed inside, and continued to extend the hole.

Material built up behind her, which she thrust away with

her feet. The thought of closing the opening to the pit horrified her, though she knew it would be inevitable.

To keep her mind off the many grim scenarios that could result from her efforts, she thought about Carina and their siblings. She hoped they were all still okay, and that she would find them soon after she escaped.

When concern for her family also threatened her composure, she turned her mind to Kamil. She'd only just begun to get to know him but she liked him a lot, and he seemed to really like her too.

She had to escape. She had to reunite with her family and with the mercs. Together, they would find a way to get off the planet.

How long was the tunnel? Was she near the surface yet?

Black, wet earth surrounded her and covered her from head to toe. She didn't dare look toward her feet in case the hole through to the pit had now closed up. She'd been steadily pushing away the dug material, but deep inside she knew that she must now be some way beyond the hole's entrance. She was like a grub, wriggling underground, trying to find the light.

Was she even digging in the right direction any longer? She thought she was, but she could have turned without realizing. She had no way to confirm which way was up and which was down, and the low gravity didn't help. She *felt* like she was digging upward, but she could be mistaken.

Grab, pull, push down past her body. Grab another handful. Kick her feet. Drag herself forward with her elbows.

The air was thick with moisture. Soil particles lined her mouth and nostrils and clogged her eyelids. Earth pressed in on her ribs and hips, and she had to force each breath, each onward movement.

Where was Carina? Where were her brothers and sisters? Where was Kamil?

What wouldn't she give to see one of them right now? What

would she not sacrifice for someone, anyone, to push a hand through the humus above her and pull her up and out?

Where was Mother? She wanted the dear, sweet, kind, tortured, sad woman, but she was gone. Gone, long ago and far away, and she would never see her again.

Fear and grief forced its way up from her stomach into her throat, and she gave a great sob. Immediately, she coughed, struggling to breathe in the scant air.

She was nearing the end of her strength. If she didn't reach the surface soon, she would never make it.

What a terrible way to go. The Regians would see what she'd done and maybe they would dig her out, and then...

A spasm of revulsion passed through her, driving her out from her fog of despair. She realized she'd stopped moving, stopped digging. How long had she been lying there?

She would not die this dreadful death, buried alive in a grave of her own making.

She would *not*!

With a last, desperate effort, she plunged her hand into the earth—and broke through into empty air!

She'd paused in her digging only a short distance below the surface.

Energy flooded into her. She pulled down the soil above, closing her eyes and spluttering in the deluge. She felt air movement on her face. For a moment, she lay still, enjoying the simple ability to breathe freely.

Caution overcame her elation, however. If she emerged from the hole in front of a Regian, all her hard work would be undone.

She waited, listening for the telltale rustle of carapaces and for the aliens' voices over her comm. No sound broke the silence.

Slowly, she lifted her head and peered out into the passage. The chitinous walls dimly shone, reflecting the soft green glow from the ceiling. She seemed to be the only living thing in the immediate area.

She pulled down more soil, and then grabbed the edges of the hole before easing herself up and out.

For the briefest moment Parthenia shook and wiped off the earth that clung to her.

Then she ran, but before she'd gone far, she stopped and ran back.

The hole she'd made gaped wide and obvious in the floor. She pulled in soil from the edges. If she'd dug a vertical tunnel, her efforts would have been useless, but she managed to fill the diagonally sloping space.

She quickly patted the earth flat, and then she was up and on her way, heading in the opposite direction to the king's chamber.

35

"Don't worry," Carina said. "We'll get out of here somehow."

She was trying to allay her siblings' fears, but her words sounded hollow even to herself. She'd thought their abilities would protect them from the worst the Regians could do, but the fact that the aliens had placed them in the same area as their other victims indicated otherwise.

Why else would they have put them there if not to attach the cases to their stomachs and leave them to die, slowly and horribly?

She was almost certain what the cases contained, and what would happen to the bodies of the people who had already died. Certain insect species used other animals as hosts for their young, laying eggs inside the living bodies. When the eggs hatched, the larva would feed on the readily available meat, which would remain fresh for as long as the host survived.

The cases were probably Regian eggs, containing one or more embryos. When the eggs hatched the embryo would burrow into the stomachs of the victims and slowly eat them from the inside out. The next stage in the growth cycle usually involved molting and then moving away to find other food sources.

Among the rotting corpses she thought she could see the shed carapaces of small Regians, as well as some kind of fungal sprouting body.

She guessed that, at an earlier point in the history of their species, the aliens had parasitized a native animal, but these original hosts had become extinct, and so the Regians had sought a replacement to fill the role. The humans newly colonizing the sector had been in the wrong place at the wrong time, and that was that.

The only thing that puzzled her was why the people they'd captured didn't appear able to get up and move around. The insects she knew of which employed that method of raising their young usually paralyzed the host with a toxin, rendering them immobile without killing them. But the people in the room could move, albeit only slightly, and their movements appeared random. She couldn't see anything holding them down.

At least they didn't appear to be in pain or fully conscious. They reminded her of the people who had suffered brain trauma and whose families couldn't afford the splicers' fee to treat them, so they remained in bed, eating and sleeping, but not really 'awake'.

Carina turned her gaze from the appalling, pitiful sight and tried to see her brothers and sisters but the place was too dark.

None of them had answered her attempt at a reassuring comment.

"Hey, guys, did you hear me?"

Her question drew short replies from each. They were still there, just too traumatized to speak.

She wished the Regians had allowed them to be together. That would have been a small comfort, and she would have been better able to distract them from the ghastly spectacle in front of them.

Even better, she thought, glancing up at the hole in the ceiling where she'd fallen, *I could have lifted them out of here.* The distance she'd fallen hadn't seemed great. If Ferne had stood on her shoulders, Darius, Nahla, and Oriana might have been able to climb right out of the hole, and Oriana could then pull Ferne up. She reckoned they all weighed about half their regular weight in the planet's gravity.

Not that it would have done Darius or Nahla much good. They wouldn't have lived long on that cold, dark planet, but perhaps it would have been a better fate than the one that now awaited them.

A *thunk* broke the silence.

Someone had landed in the cell next door.

"Parthenia?" she called out.

"No, I'm not your sister," a surly male voice replied.

"Have you seen her? Do you know where she is?"

"No idea," said the man. "Looks like I've got worse things to worry about than you being separated from the brats."

Carina knew she'd heard him before, but she couldn't put a face to the memory.

"You *are* one of the Black Dogs, right?"

"Yeah, and you're the bitch who got me into this mess."

His tone and attitude helped her make the connection. It was the merc who'd tried it on with Parthenia, the scarred man whose behavior constantly bordered on insubordination: Chandu.

"That's rich," she spat back, in no mood to tolerate his insult. "You made the choice to stay with the band. Cadwallader paid off everyone who wanted to leave."

"And spend the rest of my life hiding out from the Dirksens? Some choice."

He was exaggerating. He wasn't easily identifiable like

Cadwallader had been. A few well-told lies would have secured his safety. But she couldn't be bothered to argue.

A dreaded sound suddenly emerged from the quiet—the rustle of approaching Regians. Several of them, from the sound of it. A few moments later she saw them. Four, walking rapidly in her direction.

Her pulse quickened. Were they coming for her? Were they about to stick an egg case to her stomach and do whatever it was they did to make people vegetative?

Carina shrank back against the far wall of her cell, her courage entirely failing her.

And yet, it was better they did it to her than one of the kids. She could only hope her siblings didn't watch what became of her.

But the Regians walked past her cell and stopped at Chandu's.

"What do you want with me, you..." He let out a string of colorful expletives.

One of the aliens opened the grid.

"Get away! Leave me alone. What are you doing? Get... Arghh, what the hell's that?"

He darted from his cell and ran into the sea of human bodies. The four Regians set off in pursuit, their long legs stepping easily over the prone figures. Chandu tripped and fell, landing face first among the corpses. He must have hit one of the mushrooms too, because a cloud of spores rose into the air.

He screamed in horror and despair as the aliens caught up to him.

The sight of the spreading cloud of particles from the fungus sparked an idea in Carina's mind. She thought she might have the explanation for the near-comatose state of the human hosts.

"Kids!" she yelled. "Try not to breathe in any of that cloud in the center there. Can you see it?" Luckily, Chandu's unhappy accident was many meters distant from the cells, and the chance of inhaling the spores was remote.

Three of the Regians were holding Chandu down, one on each leg and the third pressing down on his shoulders. He flailed, but the creatures were too strong for him.

The fourth alien held a device in his front pincers—a cubic box from which a tube protruded, widening at its end. The Regian lowered the device in front of Chandu's face.

"Stop! No!" he hollered, twisting his head vigorously from side to side. "No!" A pause, then "Arghhh! What did you do? What have you done to me?" He coughed, deeply. "Eurgh! What have you done?"

The aliens stepped back, releasing him, but Chandu didn't attempt to run away. He turned onto all fours and coughed again, so strongly he sounded about to cough up his lungs. "What was that stuff?" Carina faintly heard him say. "What did you..."

He collapsed. His arms and legs moved briefly, then they were still.

The Regians moved in again and delicately removed his clothes. Next, one of them plucked an egg case from the nearest string, and pressed it onto his stomach.

Their work done, the aliens left him and walked away, high-stepping through the grisly carpet.

They were gone, and all was still again.

Carina expected some kind of response from the children to what they'd seen—expressions of their feelings, or attempts to seek reassurance—but nothing came. Silence reigned. Her siblings were simply too horrified to speak.

Another *thunk* sounded in Carina's neighboring cell, making her jump.

A second host for the Regians' young had arrived.

She prayed it was not Bryce or Jace. If she survived this ordeal, how could she live with the memory of either of them undergoing the same experience as Chandu? It would be an endless torment.

A groan and cursing emanated from the cell.

Terror exploded in Carina's heart as she recognized the voice.

"A-Atoi? Is that you?"

36

T he cold had seeped into Parthenia's bones again. She crouched, hugging herself, near the corner of a small passage that led from the main thoroughfare. At first, she'd been terrified the Regians might smell her while she waited to catch her breath and rest. She'd heard many species' sense of smell was far superior to humans', and they used it in the way people used their sight and hearing. But either the aliens' olfactory capabilities weren't great, or the earth that coated her body was masking her scent.

Several of them had passed by while she'd been sitting and resting. They carried things in their front pincers while walking on their remaining four limbs. The light was too dim to see what they were carrying, but she had the impression the objects were regular, household things, and she was in some kind of residential area, not a military or governmental place.

It seemed odd that the king lived so close to the common citizens, and she hadn't noticed anything grand or decorative in his chamber. Perhaps the Regians' society was very egalitarian, or their culture didn't value external displays of wealth or power.

Another Regian oddity struck her: they carried no weapons. They fought using the acid they produced naturally. She had to admit the strategy was effective against humans who were wearing no armor, yet it was strange that a space-faring species hadn't invented military technology. Unless they had, but it couldn't be used at close quarters?

She shivered, wondering what to do next. Trying to understand the creatures who had captured her didn't seem to be helping her to figure out how to escape from them.

One thing she knew for sure: she had to get out of that place somehow. It wouldn't be long before her guard returned to her pit and saw she was missing. She wouldn't be able to go far on foot, and the Regians would know all they had to do to recapture her again was to search for her. They certainly had the numbers to cover a wide area quickly.

But if she could leave that metropolis she might stand a chance. She might even discover where the aliens were keeping her family and the Black Dogs. If she could release them, that would really be something. The way things were at the moment, she would be content just to see a face she knew.

Deciding she'd rested enough and now she was only going to get even colder, she peeked out from her hiding place, and immediately drew her head in again. A Regian was approaching. It was impossible to hear them on the soft humus floors of their habitation.

Parthenia pressed her back against the hard, smooth wall and held her breath. The creature stopped directly outside the little alley. She froze, but not before shrinking her eyes to slits in case the white in them stood out against her besmirched skin and hair.

The Regian turned away from her, and her muscles relaxed a notch. It was doing something to the wall opposite.

As she watched, a section rose, revealing a slope of many tiny steps leading up. The Regian walked through the opening, and the section descended again. When it closed, it blended so well with the rest of the wall it was impossible to see.

Could this be an exit to the outside? The steps might only lead up to the next level, but she would be nearer her goal.

After checking no other aliens were approaching, Parthenia slipped from the alley and crossed to the wall.

How had the creature opened the exit? She hadn't noticed it carrying anything, like a key or a security device.

Her gaze scanned the surface until it alighted on a small hole at the height of her shoulders, which was about the level of the top of a Regian's limbs. She bent down and looked into the hole, but it was impossible to see anything. The dim light didn't penetrate the orifice.

Her heart beat faster. The obvious thing to do was to put a finger in, but she feared something might cut or bite it off. Swallowing, she lifted her left, non-dominant hand, and poked her index finger into the hole. A sloping surface presented itself. A switch? She pressed the uppermost part.

Click!

The section rose.

Parthenia darted in and ran up the many narrow steps. As she ran, she realized it was edges like these she'd stumbled and cut her knees on when the Regians had brought her here. Not at all suited to human feet, they were perfect for the aliens' slim pincers.

The stairs continued for about ten meters and ended with another section of wall. She quickly located the hole that held the switch and pressed it.

Beyond the open doorway stretched the desolation of the surface of the Regians' planet. An icy wind cut straight to her skin, but Parthenia ran out anyway. Groups of large and small rocks peppered the landscape. She sped to the nearest group, which were sufficiently large to hide among. She leapt over a rock at the edge, and then hunkered down.

Looking back the way she'd come, she saw a low hill with the door to the lower level set in the side. The door was closed, and the Regian she'd seen go up the stairs was nowhere in sight.

It was nighttime, but it wasn't too dark to see the barren surface clearly. The heavy clouds she'd seen earlier had cleared, and three moons shone down—one large and two smaller flanking it.

Where had the alien gone? She couldn't see any other entrances to the habitation. The creature couldn't have disappeared. It must have been going *somewhere*. Perhaps it had been on its way to the place where her family and the others had been confined.

She stood up and peered out in the other direction.

Moonlight illuminated every rock and pebble of the dusty surface. The horizon seemed close, though it was hard to get a sense of perspective in the unfamiliar scenery.

She caught her breath. Only a few meters away stood a group of five Regians. Their black carapaces were the perfect camouflage in the landscape of deep shadows cast from the three moons' beams. One of them had moved a little, attracting her attention.

They were standing facing the same direction, as if waiting for something.

Parthenia shook with cold and her teeth chattered. Standing up brought her out of the shelter of the rocks, exposing her to the biting wind. She ducked down again, knowing she was nearing the limits of her body's endurance. But returning to the comparative warmth underground was out of the question. Better to die out there, free from captivity. She only wished she'd had a chance to see her siblings and Kamil again.

She risked another peek over the rocks. The aliens remained in the same position. What could they be waiting for?

No entrances to their habitation stood nearby except the one where she'd exited, and she couldn't see any roads or buildings.

Once more, the freezing breeze got the better of her, and she sank into the lee of the rocks.

The wind soughed and whined as it rushed past. Parthenia jammed her frozen fingers into her armpits and tried to listen beyond its noise. She looked up at the three moons and unfamiliar starscape. How far was she from Ithiya now? She had no idea.

The gilded prison that had once been her home seemed distant and dreamlike. Despite the presence of her demonic father, she'd had many happy times there, playing with her brothers and sisters and enjoying the quiet, comforting love of their mother, which persisted throughout Father's moods and tirades.

She recalled the warm, verdant garden that surrounded the mansion, full of fruits and flowers. Sometimes she'd simply sat with Mother in the sun, not speaking, just soaking up the pleasant warmth. She could almost feel the sun's warmth right now, and the drowsiness that came with it. It felt wonderful. She wanted to slip into sleep, warm and secure.

Whoomph!

The noise jerked her awake, and she felt a tremor run through the ground.

Why did she feel so hot when before she'd been so cold?

And what had made that noise?

Fighting exhaustion, she rose to her feet again and looked out.

Something was there that hadn't been there before. Something huge.

Its shape reminded her of seashells that Father had once brought home, curved on one side and flat on the other, but this thing was many times larger. The tallest part stood thirty times higher than a Regian, and it was the same width. The flat section rested on the ground, and a vertical surface rose from the base to the top.

She was in no doubt the thing had landed, causing the sound and the vibration, and the size and appearance of the object would ordinarily have led her to conclude it was some kind of airplane or starship, except the thing was *alive*.

The tips at the edges of its body were moving, rippling like the fins of a flat fish, and the vertical surface at what seemed to be its front end looked soft, like skin.

The Regians who had been waiting walked toward the creature. As they got near, an opening appeared, drawing back its edges like curtains or two lips around a mouth.

Parthenia watched and waited. The Regians went inside.

The opening was a pitch black hole, giving no clue as to what was happening in there.

Time passed, though she didn't know how much. It could have been seconds or minutes. All she knew was she had to see what was happening, what this thing was that had arrived. She was at the end of her endurance and it was her only hope of survival.

Finally, the Regians emerged.

And between the five walked two men!

She squinted to make out their faces. She didn't recognize either of them, which probably meant they were Mezban's soldiers. And if they were Mezban's troops, that seemed to mean the thing they'd arrived in had brought them there from the *Bathsheba*!

An animal that flew through space? She'd vaguely heard of such creatures, but none the size of a starship, and none which also carried passengers. But she didn't have the luxury of contemplating the revelation right now.

Excitement coursed through her. If she saw where the men were taken, that might tell her where her family and the Black Dogs were being held too.

The Regians poked the men with their pincers to direct them as they'd poked her, though she noticed they weren't wearing bags over their heads as she had. What *that* meant, she didn't know.

The group walked around the huge flying creature and disappeared.

Parthenia started out from her hiding place, somewhat fearful of the living starship perceiving her and raising an alarm, but it didn't appear to react as she approached it. She followed the same path as the aliens and their captives, around the right-hand 'fin' or 'wing'. As soon as she rounded the tip, she saw the group again.

The Regians were poking the men vigorously, urging them forward, but they were resisting. Suddenly, one of the aliens gave a man a particularly hard shove, and he dropped down out of sight. A beat later the same thing happened to the other man.

The soldiers had fallen so quickly, it was clear they'd been pushed into holes in the ground. Was that what had happened to her family?

She needed to get closer to the holes and find out, but the Regians were returning!

Parthenia spun around, looking for a place to hide.

There was nothing.

No group of boulders in this area was large enough to hide her. Her only chance was to return the way she'd come.

But the aliens had already spotted her. They were loping in her direction, covering the ground fast on their lengthy limbs.

She ran.

Weighing much less than her usual weight, running should have been easy, but she had no energy left. Her legs moved as if trying to wade through treacle.

Then she fell.

A second later, a Regian loomed over her.

"No!" she yelled. "Don't take me back there! I won't go. I want to see my family. I want to be with them!"

She scrabbled backward on all fours, trying but failing to rise.

A hole opened in the front of the alien's carapace, and liquid spurted out.

Acid splashed across her exposed skin.

She shrieked in agony.

37

C arina lay on her side, unable to move, unable to think.

Atoi was gone.

Her friend was as good as dead, and her last conscious moments had been filled with terror, knowing her sickening fate.

Right now, somewhere out there among the parasitized corpses—some dead and some still living—lay the person she'd known since she'd first boarded the *Duchess* as a sixteen-year-old street rat. They'd trained, fought, and partied together, and though neither of them had ever put it into words, they'd liked and trusted each other.

After Atoi had landed in the cell next door, the woman had quickly taken in and understood the situation. Carina hadn't had to do much explaining: it didn't take a genius to figure out what the Regians intended to do to them.

Except maybe not the mages.

Chandu had been inoculated with the fungal spores as soon as he'd arrived. She was confident that was what the aliens had sprayed into the man's face. As well as several insects that lay eggs in hosts' bodies as part of their life cycle, she'd also come across individual creatures who behaved as if in a trance, wandering around in the open aimlessly, or climbing to the tops of plants and remaining exposed, as if inviting a predator to eat them.

The insects that exhibited this strange behavior all had one thing in common: a tiny protuberance on their heads like a small mushroom. They'd clearly been infested by a fungus that affected their actions. When she'd seen the puff of spores from the fungal body that Chandu crushed among the corpses, she'd understood the reason for the lack of animation in the people still alive. The Regian squirted something up Chandu's nose and into his mouth, confirming her conclusion.

The spores had quickly infiltrated the man's brain and affected his motor functions. She only hoped—nasty though Chandu was—that his mind was not awake and functioning normally trapped in an unresponsive body.

But the Regians hadn't done the same thing to the mages, yet. She supposed the aliens were delaying in the hope she and her siblings might be more useful to them than only fresh meat.

The same had not been true for Atoi. The accusation she'd thrown at Carina aboard the *Duchess* as the *Peregrine* towed it back to the colony ship had proven true. The mages were to be spared, for now, but the mercs were not to be granted the same clemency.

It would have been better for her friend if they had activated the self-destruct, and it was a sign of their friendship that she had not.

Atoi had paid the price.

"Yeah, it's me," she'd answered Carina. "That you, Car? What the freaking stars is going on in here?"

Before Carina answered, she'd added, "Or maybe I don't

want to know. *Fuck*. What happened to Chandu? I saw them bring him here ahead of me."

She replied quietly, "He's out there."

Atoi was silent.

Carina could hear her friend's breaths, heavy and speeding up, in the stillness.

"Guess they'll be coming for me soon," she said.

Carina couldn't answer her.

"You know what I said, on the *Duchess*?" she asked, "about you mages and us mercs?"

"Uh huh."

"I didn't mean it. I want you to forget about it."

"But you were—"

"Forget it, okay!?"

"Okay," Carina replied, though she knew she never would.

She heard Atoi stand up and grip the cage wires.

"And keep working out, right? You're weak. You can be stronger, and you need to be to protect those brats."

"You know, the Regians came for Chandu faster than this. Maybe—"

Four aliens appeared from the shadows and strode toward Atoi's cell.

Her friend muttered expletives, then she said, "Car, promise me something."

"*Anything.*"

"Make it worth it. Live a good life. A long life, for me."

The sobs that were choking Carina stole her reply.

The Regians opened Atoi's cell door.

She'd put up a helluva fight, breaking two of the aliens' legs and nearly making it to the exit before they caught her and managed to subdue her.

And the result had been the same. Atoi lay somewhere out there, not yet dead but not quite living, and Carina would never be the same again.

Since then, more Black Dogs had been arriving, but the aliens seemed to be leaving them alone for now. The men and women occupied most of the cells around the perimeter of the hatching chamber. Carina had broken the news about Atoi and Chandu. The mercs had been distressed and saddened by hearing the fate of their captain, but Chandu's death went unremarked.

Even if she had elixir, a Heal Cast wouldn't fix what had happened to her friend. It couldn't drive the spores out from her body any more than it could remove a knife from her stomach, and spores were far too small to Transport.

At first, she and the mercs had discussed escape strategies, but no one had come up with anything concrete. Now, the noise in the place was minimal. Each of them kept their thoughts to themselves, though she could hear murmurings that could be prayers.

She heard the impact on the floor of a new person arriving, but the noise barely penetrated her misery.

There was a silence as the new arrival took in the shocking sight before them, but then a voice called out, "Carina, are you here?"

Bryce.

She sat up. "I'm here."

She could just see him, looking out from a cell a few meters away.

"And the kids?"

"We're here, too," Ferne replied. "Though we don't know where Parthenia is."

"Are you all okay?"

"Yeah," Oriana replied sadly. "We're fine."

"Atoi's dead," said Carina. "The Regians took her...out there."

"*Shit.* I'm sorry. I know you and she were friends."

Carina couldn't respond.

"There has to be a way out of this," Bryce said.

"I'm all ears," one of the mercs growled.

"We haven't any elixir," said Oriana. "If we had just a little, a mouthful, maybe we could do something."

"But we don't," said Ferne, "so there's no point wishing."

Another *thunk!*

Another awful silence, each person in the room knowing what the new person was going through.

Carina watched the place the Regians had come from before. The cells were nearly full. How long would the aliens wait before they returned to select the next host?

In some ways, it might be better to be chosen soon, if the only alternative was to sit and see what would become of you. If the Regians decided the mages were of no use to them, they would probably be the last to be chosen. Carina wasn't sure they were better off.

Someone cleared their throat—a deep, male cough.

"Carina Lin, are you in here?"

She sighed. "Yes, Jace. I'm here."

"Good. And the rest of your family?"

"We're missing Parthenia," Ferne replied.

"Ah, that's unfortunate."

"Is it?" Carina asked. "I was hoping she was in a better place than this."

"Yes, it is. It means we'll have to find her."

"I'd love to find her, but I've no idea how."

A pause.

"Is this place under surveillance by the aliens?" Jace asked.

"I don't think so," Carina replied. "Why?"

"I have something for you, for us, but I'm not sure if it's safe to talk about it."

"Something for me?" She stood up and peered across the room, trying to see the older mage.

His large figure was easy to spot.

"Yes, something very useful, though not much of it."

"Something..." Carina's legs became weak, and she grasped the wires for support. "You're *kidding* me!"

"I'm not joking. Er...perhaps I shouldn't say any more, now we understand each other."

The Regians didn't know Jace was a mage. Lomang and Mezban hadn't told them because *they* hadn't known! And because none of the mercs had been wearing armor, he'd been mistaken for one of them. After the *Duchess* was seized, the Black Dogs' weapons had been collected, but no one had seen any reason to take away a soldier's canteen.

Jace was carrying elixir.

38

The sound of the cell doors unlocking was like the ratchet of a hundred insect legs rubbing together on a still night.

If their supply of elixir had been plentiful, they might have Transported all the mercs out of the hatching chamber, but they didn't. And even if they did, where should the mercs go? No one knew of a safe place on the Regians' planet.

The Unlock Cast required little effort and Jace could accomplish it with only one mouthful of the precious fluid.

Now they were free, the Black Dogs moved into action. One ran into his neighbor's cell and called for another's help. The three men quickly formed a tower in the hole that led to the surface, and the topmost man looked out.

Immediately, he dropped to the floor and said in a loud whisper, "Regians, coming this way."

Carina swore. "Quick, back in your cells, everyone. If they come in here, I'll Split them."

But the aliens didn't enter the chamber. Instead, new victims dropped into empty cells—two of Mezban's soldiers.

What their arrival meant was unclear, but a quick decision

had to be made. As the men were boggling at the sight of the dead and dying human hosts, one of the mercs sped over to them and demanded to know where their loyalty lay. Would they forsake Mezban and come over to the mercenary band?

Unsurprisingly, the soldiers agreed, giving loud assurances of their new fealty.

"Let's go!" said Carina, as loudly as she dared.

As she ran to reunite with Bryce and gather her brothers and sisters, the Black Dogs began to form towers as the original three had.

The first men and women climbed up and out.

Carina quickly stepped through the dreadful blanket of human hosts in the center of the chamber. When she reached Atoi, she stopped. Her friend's eyes were open, though unfocused, and her chest slowly rose and fell. The swollen egg case covered more than half of the woman's torso. Carina saw movement through the translucent shell—something wriggling.

"I'm sorry," she whispered, kneeling down.

Her heart and throat aching like they were about to burst, she gently took her friend's head in both hands, and then twisted it sharply. A crack of breaking bone sounded, and Atoi's neck hung loose.

The rising and falling of her chest stopped, and her eyes closed.

For a moment, Carina couldn't see. Her tears dripped onto her old friend's face. "Goodbye," she murmured. "Thanks for all you did, all you were."

Then a scream from outside pierced the air. The person's voice was alarmingly familiar.

"That's Parthenia!" Carina yelled. She ran out from the hosts and over to Jace, grabbing the elixir from him before speeding on to the nearest tower of mercs.

"Help me up!" she shouted, pushing the canteen down her shirt.

The waiting mercs parted before her, and the man at the bottom formed a stirrup with his hands. She put her foot on it, he boosted her upward, and the next man grabbed her wrists, lifting her higher. In another second she was pulling herself out of the hole and onto the cold, dusty surface of the Regian planet.

Blinking in the bright moonlight, she swiveled, scanning the landscape. The first thing she saw was the slope of a small, dark hill—except it wasn't a hill, unless hills moved. The lower reaches of the slope were undulating. She seemed to be looking at a living creature.

Then she saw the Regians. Five of them were gathered around something on the ground.

Another scream rent the atmosphere.

Carina's hands shook as she pulled the canteen out from her shirt and unscrewed the lid. She steadied her breath, took a drink, and closed her eyes. Achieving the calmness of mind required to Cast was hard, but failing wasn't an option in the circumstances.

She opened her eyes. The five Regians briefly shrieked before they were torn in two and their bodies evaporated into the ether. As she raced to her sister, she hoped the aliens' death throes hadn't been heard by others of their kind.

Parthenia was a ball of grime and burned flesh, curled up on her side on the ground.

"I've got you," Carina sobbed, cradling her sister. "I've got you."

She sipped elixir again and quickly Cast Heal.

While she watched fresh skin grow over Parthenia's wounds, some mercs arrived at her side.

"We're bringing the rest of your family," one of them said.

The tension in Parthenia's body faded, and she sat up. "Thank you."

"Thank the stars you're okay," Carina replied, rubbing the wetness from her eyes with the heel of her hand.

More mercs were running up, followed by Jace, Ferne, and Darius.

"Where are Oriana and Nahla?" asked Carina.

"They're coming with Bryce," Jace replied, "but we need to Transport the last of the soldiers up here. They can't get out by themselves.

Carina shook the canteen. Very little elixir remained, but leaving anyone behind was out of the question. She handed the canteen to Jace, who took it and left.

"Now what?" Ferne asked.

She was distracted from answering his question by the look in Darius's eyes. The boy's gaze was tortured and he looked as though he were in pain. Of all the experiences her brother had endured, Carina doubted he would ever recover from this one.

"We could try to steal the Regians' ship," Parthenia replied.

"That would be ideal," said Carina, "if we knew where they kept them."

"It's right there." Parthenia pointed at the hillock.

Carina turned to take in the sight of the massive animal again. "That's a *starship*? Are you feeling all right?"

"I heard it land, and I saw the Regians bring two of Mezban's soldiers out of it."

Was *that* why the aliens had put bags over their heads? To prevent the mages from seeing how they traveled between the stars? Their precaution was certainly justified. An organic, living space vessel could have many advantages over the regular kind.

"Then we'll try," Carina said.

Jace was returning with the remaining mercs, and in the meantime, Oriana and Nahla had also arrived with Bryce.

She explained as quickly as she could what was proposed,

and then set off at a run with Parthenia, who took her to the entrance to the vessel.

A tall facade rose to a narrow overhang above.

"That's the opening," said Parthenia, indicating a cleft at the base.

"Gross!" Ferne exclaimed. "It's like lips." He prodded the surface. "Feels like skin!"

"Should we Cast Open?" asked Oriana.

But as she spoke the aperture opened.

"Quick, inside," Carina urged.

A hefty merc held her back, then nodded at a couple of others. The two soldiers ran in, followed by the man who'd made her wait.

He re-emerged. "All clear."

"Regians!" someone shouted.

The aliens were pouring from a doorway a short distance away.

"Should we Split them?" asked Ferne.

"Not if we can avoid it," she replied, hoping to conserve the vital elixir.

The mercs were running into the living starship. A couple had picked up Darius and Nahla and were carrying them in. Ferne and Oriana disappeared into the opening.

"C'mon," said Jace, tugging on her arm.

"Just a minute. I have to..."

"What?"

Carina's heart was torn. The remaining elixir could make all the difference, and yet she couldn't leave the Regian planet without doing one last thing.

She swigged elixir.

"What are you doing?!" Jace demanded.

She closed her eyes and Cast.

When she opened them again, the Regians were nearly

upon them, and Jace was standing at the entrance to the starship, beckoning her urgently.

She looked toward the holes in the ground that led to the hatching chamber.

Flames were already licking from them.

39

As Carina stepped into the Regians' starship, Oriana took the elixir from her and Cast Lock on the door... and Darius seemed to be in agony.

The little boy was writhing on the floor. "It hurts! It hurts! It hurts!"

Ferne and Jace were kneeling at his side, but they didn't seem able to help him.

"What's wrong?" Carina asked, crouching down. "What's wrong, sweetheart?"

"He doesn't appear to have any injuries," said Jace.

"Darius," said Ferne, placing a hand on his brother's forehead, "what hurts?"

"Should I Cast Heal on him anyway?" asked Parthenia.

"Maybe, but..." Carina had a feeling there was another explanation for Darius's state. "Where's the pain coming from? Is it from somewhere on your body, or...?"

"No, not me," he gasped. "The animal! The animal hurts bad."

A merc ran up, emerging from the ship's interior. "We're screwed. We can't find the flight controls."

Carina cursed. Stealing an alien ship had always been a long shot, now it looked like they were out of chances.

Darius sat up, sweating and gasping, his eyes wide. He clasped Carina's arm. "You have to help it! You have to help the animal."

There was only one animal around there she knew about.

"The ship?" she asked. "Is that the animal you mean?"

Her brother dug his fingers into her flesh. "You have to take off the tie. It hurts so much."

A faint drumming could be heard from outside. The Regians were trying to get in. The Lock Cast would hold for a while but not forever, and she was worried the aliens would spray acid on the starship creature.

"What tie?" she asked. "Do you know where it is?"

It was a long shot, but perhaps fixing the starship's problem might help them with their plight. It certainly couldn't do them any harm.

"Uh huh," Darius nodded, grimacing.

Carina helped him stand, and then supported him as he set off into the opening that yawned beyond the wide entrance.

Her brother walked like he carried the weight of an entire planet on his shoulders, wincing and letting out small groans as he went along. He hobbled down a passage that resembled a throat—slim supporting ribs underlying the translucent, pale green 'skin' of the walls and ceiling that curved over them.

A hole in the wall appeared on one side.

"Down there," said Darius. "It's down there."

The tunnel that led from the hole sloped steeply. If they went down it, Carina wasn't sure how they would get up again. They would have to Transport, and that would take the last of the elixir.

Still, there seemed nothing else she could do, and perhaps the flight controls were down there.

"Okay," she said. "Come here."

She sat on the edge of the hole and pulled her brother onto her lap.

She pushed off with one hand, and they slid down the strange facsimile of something from a children's playground.

The Regians had embedded their phosphorescent plant on the ceiling of the tunnel, unless it grew there naturally, which Carina doubted. The illumination lit their way as they smoothly descended. If Darius hadn't been in pain and they hadn't been in dire danger of recapture by the Regians, it might have been fun.

They hit the bottom.

"Ow! Ow! Ow!" Darius yelled, though it couldn't have been due to the mild impact.

"Is the tie here?" asked Carina.

They were inside a roughly round room, the skin of its walls stretched over supporting ribs as it had been in the passage and tunnel. Structures protruding from the walls slotted together like pieces of a 3D puzzle.

"Yeah, it's here! There! There it is!" He ran a few steps to one of the structures and grabbed at something frantically.

"Let me see," said Carina, joining him.

Darius moved a little to one side, but his small hands didn't leave the thing he was clasping.

It was a binding of a tough, flexible material tied tightly around a piece of the starship's tissue that bent like an elbow.

Her brother was plucking uselessly at the ligature.

"Darius, you have to move out of the way so I can try to untie it."

He let go and stepped back, wringing his hands.

Carina squatted down and examined the binding from above and then below. When she looked at the underside it was clear to see how the material had simply been twisted tightly together and knotted. She worked her fingers into the knot and pulled it apart, and then she quickly untwisted the tie. The tie hung loose.

"Uhhh," said Darius, flopping to the floor. "That's better."

"It's stopped hurting now?"

"Yeah." He put his head in his hands. "That hurt so much."

"I thought it was only emotions you felt?" Carina asked.

"I do, but when people are in pain they get upset too."

The floor suddenly lurched. She gripped one of the structures to keep her balance, but the movement was too great. She landed next to her brother.

"What was that?" asked Darius.

"I was hoping you could tell me."

The starship lurched again, and then came the distinct feeling that they were rising.

"Are we going up?" Darius asked.

"I think so. Are we? How does the starship feel?"

"It's happy now. *Much* happier. I think it's flying!"

The floor lifted and turned, sending them barreling into a corner. Then it turned again, sending them in the opposite direction. Darius squealed and then giggled. "This is fun!"

The sensation of rising continued. There could be no doubt, they *were* flying. Removing the starship creature's binding seemed to have released the Regians' control of it, and now it was escaping, taking its occupants with it.

"Carina!" called a voice from the other end of the tunnel.

"That's Ferne," said Darius.

"I know." She went to the opening. "We're down here!"

A moment later, Ferne's voice came echoing down, louder: "*There* you are. We've been looking everywhere for you. Do you know we took off from the planet?"

"Yes, we realized."

"Oh. Well, we found the rest of Mezban's soldiers. They were corralled together in a big room."

"Are Lomang and Mezban with them?"

"Uh huh. And the big guy. But the soldiers are really angry with them. They figured out they could have gotten away from the Regians if Mezban and Lomang hadn't taken them back to the *Bathsheba*. And the two that have sworn allegiance to the Black Dogs are talking to them. Things are getting a bit hot in there."

"Honestly, that sounds like good news to me," Carina replied, calling up the tunnel. If Mezban's troops dealt with her, her husband, and her husband's brother, it meant she wouldn't have to. She was too tired for revenge.

"How are you two going to get out of there?" Ferne asked.

"Um, I'm not sure."

"Should I ask Jace to Transport you?"

"No, it's a waste of elixir. We need to save it for an emergency."

"Well, I'll see if I can find a rope or something."

"Thanks."

"No problem." Ferne paused, then said, "Do you know where the starship's taking us?"

"Nope. I have no idea."

"Okay. I just thought I would ask."

40

They were heading for a moon.

Bryce wrapped his arm around Carina as they sat behind the transparent shield covering one of the starship's four openings to space. The openings appeared to be part of the creature's vision organs. Sensitive sprays of tissue stood behind each shield, but there was also a space wide enough for two people, and the creature didn't seem too bothered by them sitting there.

Carina rested her head on Bryce's shoulder and looked out at the Regian planet's three moons, floating serenely in a sea of star-speckled ink. The moons were slowly growing larger, and there was no longer any doubt they were the starship's destination. The central, largest one seemed the likeliest target.

Bryce gently squeezed her. "How are you feeling?"

She sighed. "I miss Atoi."

"We all do," Bryce said softly. "She was tough, but she was well-liked."

"She was..."

What to say? Atoi had been her bunk mate, her friend, and her savior on more than one occasion when they'd worked together as mercs. Cadwallader's death had been hard, but Carina hadn't shared the same instinctive understanding with him as she had with her old friend. The woman would have a place in Carina's heart forever.

"She was...?" Bryce reminded her.

"I can't talk about her yet." She sighed again. "We need to figure out what to do when we reach that moon."

"Do you think the starship's going to land and eject us?"

"Who knows? But I don't think so. I think she carries around other creatures in a kind of symbiotic relationship. She gets some benefit from our presence, though I haven't figured out what that is, and her passengers get to travel into space. The Regians probably hitched rides on them for millenia until one day they discovered a way to control them and force them to go to destinations of their choosing."

"*She*?" Bryce asked.

"All starships are female. You should know that by now."

"Okay. We need to persuade *her* to take us to the *Bathsheba*."

"Yeah, but how? My fear is that she's attracted to the light of the moon, and when she gets there, she'll be attracted to the light of the Regian planet and fly right back."

"Ugh, I hope not."

"Me too. But at least we'll be prepared this time. We might not have any weapons or armor or elixir, but..." Carina's words petered out. The kids had searched the ship high and low for ingredients to make elixir and a fire, but they'd found nothing.

"You're not filling me with optimism here," said Bryce.

She sighed and settled her head a little more.

"Bryce, I want to take back what I said that time in the *Bathsheba's* viewing dome."

"I kinda thought you did."

"I was cut up about the mess of pain I seem to cause the people I love. I don't want to hurt you."

"I know. I understood where you were coming from, but I

knew there wasn't anything I could say that would change your mind, so I left it. I didn't sweat it because I knew you would be back one day."

"What made you think that?"

"I'm just too irresistible."

Carina snorted and laughed before turning and pushing him away.

Bryce held out his arms, and she settled into them again.

"Cadwallader told me once, I should hold onto what I have," she said, "and I'm going to do that. Life's too short."

Live a good life. A long life, for me, Atoi had said.

If only it were that simple, but she would try, starting with not pushing away the people who meant so much to her.

They had been underway for an hour or longer. Carina was warm and her family was finally safe—for the time being, anyway. Mental and emotional exhaustion began to hit her, and she felt her eyes closing and her mind retreating to the haven of sleep.

Then the starship abruptly veered up and left, accelerating fast.

"Whoa!" she exclaimed, trying to steady herself. "What the hell?"

Shouts and cries of shock and fear echoed through from other regions of the ship.

Bryce got up and leaned out of the small recess, trying to see what was happening. The ship was continuing to pile on speed.

"Maybe the Regians are on our tail," Carina said. "They probably have more of these space-faring creatures. This one might be trying to get away from them."

She listened to the yelling but she couldn't make out what it was about.

Saying he would go and investigate, Bryce stepped down from the recess and disappeared.

While he was gone, the starship's flight gradually evened out and the creature slowed down to her previous speed.

Several minutes later, Bryce returned. He leaned in at the opening to the recess, looking pale and shaken. "Lomang and Mezban and some of the soldiers have gone!"

"What?"

"Some of the people on board aren't here anymore. One minute they were hanging out with their friends, and the next —empty space. It happened a split second before the ship switched course. "

"*Huh?!*" Fear clutched Carina's heart. "What about the kids?"

"They're okay. They're all still aboard, and Jace is too. But Lomang, Mezban, six of the Black Dogs, and roughly the same number of Mezban's ex-soldiers have vanished. Hsiao took a head count of the mercs."

He climbed in next to her and sat down.

What was going on?

What if the same thing happened again?

What could they do to stop it?

"Do you think the starship made them disappear?" Bryce asked.

"But how?" asked Carina, then she added, "I guess it's possible. Lots of things seem to happen around these parts that you don't see elsewhere."

Then Carina remembered the weird anomalous readings she'd seen on the *Duchess's* scan data while they'd been trying to escape from the Regians the first time. The ship's computer hadn't been able to interpret information that the scanners had picked up on an area of space near the Regian planet, which could only mean something about the region didn't conform with the known laws of physics.

"Oh, wow," she said, as an idea hit her. The Regians' odd

ability to time-shift, the strange composition of their bodies, the way they disappeared when they died—it all made sense.

"I think the missing people might have moved out of synch with time," she said, "or they were moved *by* something. Imagine if you suddenly stopped moving forward in time, or you moved ahead a fraction of a second, while you were aboard a vessel traveling at high speed. As soon as you re-entered normal time, the ship wouldn't be in the same place anymore."

"Moved out of synch with time?" Bryce frowned. "What are you talking about?"

Carina explained her theory, adding, "The starship knows about the anomaly. She *felt* it approach, and she flew out of its path, but not fast enough to save everyone."

"So the Regians evolved their time-shift ability due to this anomaly in space periodically drifting across their planet?"

"Exactly."

Bryce was silent, apparently digesting the concept. Eventually, he said, "I sure hope this ship detects the anomaly earlier next time."

"Me too. Those poor men and women," she said sadly.

She leaned against him again, trying to savor the moment, not knowing if it might be their last.

But the minutes crept by and nothing happened. The living starship swept through space, smoothly and sedately. It seemed like they were out of danger for now.

However, they still had no clue what to do when they reached the moon. They couldn't leave the starship, that was for sure, not on an airless asteroid. So if she decided to fly back to the planet they would have to go with her. And then what would happen?

As Carina was ruminating on their predicament, Oriana's head popped up above the edge of the opening to the recess.

"I have an idea," she announced.

"Cool," Carina replied. "What is it?"

"It's an idea about how we can get back to the *Bathsheba*."

"Even cooler," said Bryce.

"But it'll use up the last of the elixir," Oriana went on. "Jace says there's only enough for one more Cast, and I don't know if my idea will work."

"There's only one way we can find out," said Carina. "Let's hear it."

"We know the starship's alive, right? Darius could feel her pain. She thinks, and she feels, and I think she *must* make decisions about what she does and where she goes. She has a mind, that means that we, as mages, might be able to control her."

Carina gasped and sat bolt upright. "Stars, Oriana, you're right! Why didn't I think of it? One of us could Enthrall her and tell her to take us to the *Bathsheba*. She would know the ship's position because she's been there before."

"I mean, it's a little cruel..." said Oriana.

"Not as cruel as what the Regians were doing to her," Carina said, "and, once we arrived, we would set her free."

"I think you're forgetting something," Bryce said. "The *Bathsheba* might still be infested with Regians."

"Perhaps," Carina agreed, "but if we can just reach our supply of elixir, and the soldiers can get to their weapons and armor, I'm sure we can take her back again. The Regians are just insects with a unique ability who happened to have access to space-faring animals. It was Lomang and Mezban's stupidity and greed that let us down before."

Bryce smiled. "And after we take her back, then what?"

"Then we find out where we are and what year we're in, and set a course for Earth."

**CARINA LIN'S STORY CONTINUES IN
FLIGHT FROM SANCTUARY**

Printed in Great Britain
by Amazon